My Cat Nap

Middlemarch Shifters 12

Shelley Munro

My Cat Nap

Copyright © 2023 by Shelley Munro

Print ISBN: 978-1-99-106315-1
Digital ISBN: 978-0-9941433-0-3

Editor: Mary Moran

Cover: Kim Killion, The Killion Group

Munro Press, New Zealand.

First Munro Press electronic publication December 2016

First Munro Press print publication February 2023

For Paul.

INTRODUCTION

KIRAN IS A TIGER shifter without a past. Plucked from a hospital by Rohan and Ambar Patel, he has no recollection of arriving in Auckland, New Zealand. Nothing is familiar, but he's sure of one thing. Rohan Patel is an attractive man. He fires Kiran with longing. A stolen kiss and Kiran knows precisely what he wants.

Rohan's desire for the stranger steals his breath and pushes forward his plans to tell his sister he prefers males. Hurried embraces lead to an understanding, their growing relationship exhilarating. The urgent hunger between them is palpable, guaranteed to make any tiger purr with pleasure.

But weird flashes of memory hint at Kiran's terrible past. The truth might blow apart his blossoming romance with Rohan and hurt his new Middlemarch friends. A dilemma—push Rohan away or hold him close and place his lover in danger. It's a difficult choice, then it's too late. Danger stalks through Middlemarch, and they must fight for their love and their lives.

CHAPTER ONE

"ROHAN, YOU HAVE TO come right now!" Ambar skated to a halt in the doorway of their West Auckland grocery store and stared at his customer in consternation. "Um, hello, Mrs. McPherson," his sister said. "How are you?"

"Was there anything else you needed today, Mrs. McPherson?" Rohan Patel asked, ignoring Ambar's dramatic arrival. Their parents had believed in excellent customer service and enforced the principle with their children until it became second nature.

"No, thank you, dear," the elderly lady said. "How much do I owe you?"

"Ten dollars and twenty cents," Rohan answered and waited for her to dig misshapen hands deep into her cloth bag to find her purse. Ever since he could remember, the elderly lady had shopped at his parents' store. Both he and Ambar had practiced waiting on her until they'd perfected the standard of service his parents expected. In his peripheral vision, he noticed Ambar's frantic gesturing and frowned, the training of years hard to shake.

"I'll miss you when you leave. Where did you say you were going?" Mrs. McPherson asked.

"Ambar and I have purchased a business in the South Island, a place in Middlemarch." Rohan couldn't wait to move to the country with all the open land, the mountains, and the freedom to run during their leisure time. It would be great to have the sign above their new store bearing their names instead of their parents, to know they worked for themselves.

"It won't be the same without you. Your parents were lovely. I suppose it must be difficult without them?"

"Yes, it is hard, which is why we decided to start again in fresh surroundings. Ambar will help you carry your shopping out to your car," Rohan said, frowning at Ambar in clear displeasure, his older-brother-knows-best face in place. This was still their parents' store even if they owned it on paper now.

Ambar's eyes narrowed. "But—"

"Ambar." Rohan's voice held a warning, and the faint tensing of her shoulders told him she'd received the threat. Customers came first. Always. Their parents' philosophy drummed into them over the years was the reason the store remained popular with the locals.

Rohan watched Ambar tamp down her frustration. She nodded and picked up Mrs. McPherson's two bags of purchases. Silently she held the door open and waited for the woman to lumber through, the tap of her walking stick on the floor and pavement outside marking her unsteady progress. The second the car door closed after the elderly woman, Ambar darted back into the store. She flipped the lock and put the *Back in ten minutes* sign in the window.

"Rohan, we have to hurry. I saw another shifter. He was hurt, and they put him into an ambulance."

Alarm shot through Rohan. "Hell, why didn't you say so?" A shifter helpless in human hands, even if they meant well, could spell disaster. The last thing any feline wanted was a life of imprisonment and intrusive study.

Ambar sniffed and rolled her golden-brown eyes. "You didn't give me a chance."

"Do you know where they're taking him?"

"Auckland Hospital. What are we going to do?"

Rohan grabbed his wallet. "I don't know, but we can't let them do tests on him. What sort of shifter?"

"Tiger, I think, although I'm not one hundred percent sure. He was big enough. It all happened so quickly I didn't have a chance to scent him properly. He looked out of it. Before they shut the ambulance doors, he opened his eyes. I don't think anyone else saw his eyes shift except me."

Rohan hurried through the store, past the jams and breakfast cereals aisle, to the rear door. "We're the only tigers around here. Most of them live over on the north shore. Are you sure?"

"I'm not sure of anything. As I said, it was over in minutes. Maybe I'm mistaken because his skin was lighter than ours." Ambar snatched her car keys from the top of the desk in their small office as she passed. "We can discuss this once we have him safe. You know what will happen when his test results come back from the lab." She thrust the keys at her brother. "You drive. You're faster than me."

They hurried out the rear exit, locking the door after them. Rohan yanked open the car door and jumped behind the wheel.

"I can't believe you're letting me drive," Rohan said, lips quirking in silent laughter while he pulled out onto the main road.

"Just hurry. You didn't see him. I did. I wouldn't wish admittance to a public hospital on any shifter." She shuddered, and Rohan could see her mind leaping to all sorts of scenarios. "We need to come up with a plan."

"You realize I'll give you a hard time if this turns out to be a waste of time."

"I don't care," Ambar retorted. "At least this way I can live with my conscience. I'd never forgive myself if I let a fellow shifter suffer—" She slapped her hand against the dashboard to catch herself as Rohan skidded around a corner. "Go easy. The last thing we need is a cop stopping us for speeding."

Rohan heeded the warning, slowing a fraction but still driving over the speed limit. They reached the hospital and spent fifteen frustrating minutes looking for parking. Finally they found a spot and hurried into the emergency department.

"How are we going to handle this?" Ambar whispered before they neared the desk.

"Let me do the talking," Rohan said. "And start thinking about JoJo."

Ambar drew a sharp breath, tears filling her eyes when he mentioned her beloved cat. Jojo had died of old age at the end of last year, only weeks after their parents lost their lives in a fatal car crash. "Jojo?"

"Perfect," Rohan said. "Excuse me. We've just heard our brother Jojo was hurt in some sort of an accident. Can we see him?"

A sob escaped Ambar, and Rohan felt a flicker of guilt for using her in this way. She'd loved that cat. It had taken a long time for her to gain Jojo's trust because he'd sensed their shifter genes. Rohan would have given up but Ambar hadn't.

"What is his surname?"

"Jojo Patel," Rohan said smoothly. "Although he might not know his name. He has blackouts sometimes. He's tall like us. He takes after our mother and his skin is fairer." Rohan crossed his fingers and hoped the stranger really was tall.

"Let me check," she said, picking up a phone.

Ambar sniffed and shot him a quick look of approval for his fast thinking. Rohan hid a grin because, initially after their parents' death, they'd argued about moving from the city to the country. She'd told him he was dim-witted with no original thoughts to rub together inside his head. Leave the thinking to her because she did a better job.

Luckily, after more discussion she'd come to accept their move to Middlemarch wasn't such a bad one. Personally, he thought it was the large male-female ratio in Middlemarch that had swung Ambar's decision from negative to positive. Rohan had argued they needed to start over and living amongst other shifters would be a great start. There were too many of their parents' friends in Auckland who would judge them and try to offer unwanted advice.

Besides, Rohan had heard people in Middlemarch were more liberal when it came to same-sex relationships. He might even find the guts to admit his liking for males to his sister. A true fresh start. It would be good to run through the countryside on a regular basis instead of slinking around in the dark of Western Springs reserve when the need to shift became too much for them. Good thing they were on the same page.

"You can go through," the woman said. "The nurse will show you the way." She picked up a chart, and called, "Mr. James, you can go with the nurse."

They waited for the patient to follow the nurse before trailing them. Rohan sensed the uneasiness in his sister, the same tension lurking inside him. The smells and the sounds of the hospital were full of despair, the atmosphere sorrowful and downright depressing. This was dangerous. They both knew it, yet neither of them considered turning away from a fellow shifter in need.

"Can you smell anything?" Ambar whispered.

"Hospitals," Rohan replied, his eyes watchful as they passed patients on stretchers and caught glimpses of others inside curtained cubicles.

Ambar wrinkled her nose while Rohan tried to ignore the pungent scent of cleaning materials and sickness. Despondency. He could think of at least ten other places he'd rather spend his day.

"In here," the nurse said with a smile and a quick gesture. "We're waiting for a doctor to see him again. It shouldn't be much longer."

Again. That didn't sound good. Rohan pulled the curtain aside, allowing a first glimpse of the man lying on the narrow stretcher bed. "Is that him?"

The man was attached to a monitor, and Rohan presumed it was to observe his heart rate and blood pressure. Maybe his oxygen. They'd also set up a drip, which might make things tricky when they tried to get him out of the hospital. On the plus side, the medical staff didn't seem to be all over him, which meant they hadn't found anything too suspicious.

Ambar stepped closer to the bed. "Yeah. Wow, he's prettier than I remember."

Despite the gravity of the situation, brother and sister grinned at each other.

"He sure is," Rohan whispered, moving up beside her and letting the curtain fall back into place, mesmerized by the straight nose and faint beard. His hair was black and a bit unkempt. It didn't detract from his attractiveness, his dark eyelashes a silky fan below his eyes. Rohan wished he could see what color his eyes were. Ambar hadn't said, and he didn't like to ask.

He was a big man, although he appeared as if he might have been sick and hadn't recovered the weight he'd lost because the T-shirt swamped him. At peak fitness he'd look spectacular. Muscular. The stranger's sensual lips attracted Rohan's attention next, and he had to shake his carnal thoughts free before his body reacted and Ambar noticed.

"What do you think?" Ambar asked, her humor fading while she studied the stranger.

"That I wouldn't stand a chance of finding a partner if I hung out with him." Rohan leaned closer and wrinkled his nose, drawing the man's scent through his mouth and baring his teeth at the same time. The comical action helped him determine if the man was a tiger or something else. They weren't that far removed from their tiger cousins in their behavior, although they were more sociable.

Hospital smells. Laundry powder. Antiseptic wipes. Sweat and the underlying musk of man and wild tiger.

Rohan grunted and took the man's wrist, almost dropping it when he experienced an unexpected frisson of pleasure. "Tiger," he said tersely. "How the hell are we going to get him out of here? And where did he come from? We would have heard if any of the North Shore tigers had a visiting relative. We would've received a summons to attend a welcome party."

The rapid slap-slap of rubber-soled shoes on the hard floor stopped directly outside and the curtain whipped open. A young woman wearing jeans and a buttoned white hospital coat stepped inside. A stethoscope hung around her neck.

"Are you family?" she asked.

"Our brother," Rohan said easily. He smoothed the man's dark hair away from his face, strangely reluctant to lose contact with the stranger. "JoJo."

Rohan took a calming breath and smiled. With his tall, muscular build and his golden-brown eyes, women adored him. Men too. *Lucky for him.* The mixed blood in their background, that of European and Eastern Indian, had favored both with above-average looks. Sometimes their physical appearance came in handy. Ambar winked at him, and he could practically read her thoughts. The woman wouldn't stand a chance if he turned on the charm.

"The ambulance crew said he had a seizure and collapsed." The woman tugged up the dirty T-shirt he wore and lifted her stethoscope to listen to his heart. "He seems stable. All the tests we've done indicate he's okay, but I'm worried because he hasn't regained consciousness. We're going to admit him to ICU for more tests." She frowned, pausing to listen again. "Weird," she muttered.

"Is something wrong, doctor?" Rohan asked.

"His heart...he has a heart murmur." Her face cleared. "Were you aware of that?"

Rohan glanced at Ambar and came to a quick decision. "No, is that a problem?"

The doctor shook her head. "A lot of people have heart murmurs and lead normal lives. I'm sending him to the ICU ward. Ah, here is the porter to take him now. You can go with him if you want."

Ambar leaned closer to Rohan and whispered in his ear. "What are we going to do? I wonder which tests they've done. If they've taken blood we're in trouble."

Rohan waited until the woman moved on to her next patient before answering. "A blood test is pretty standard when they're not sure what's happening. We have to get

11

him out of here. Hopefully, it won't be as difficult if he's in a room."

"If he disappears they won't have any reason to look at the test results," Ambar said. "They're busy and that might work in our favor, but the staff will be everywhere in the ICU. It's not going to be easy."

"That's true." And unhooking him from the machines wouldn't be easy either.

They hurried to catch up, entering the elevator with the porter and the stranger, still on the stretcher bed. Five minutes later they entered a ward, the porter skillfully maneuvering the bed, the portable monitor and the drip.

"In the far room," a harried nurse said after checking the stranger's chart. "A nurse will attend to him in a few minutes."

"You're lucky this room is empty," the porter said, directing them to a room at the end of the corridor. "It will fill up tonight. Friday nights and weekends are busy around here." He left them with a wave.

"I repeat, what are we going to do? He's not even conscious," Ambar said. "We can't exactly steal the bed, and won't those machines beep when we remove everything?"

"We're gonna have to risk it. Maybe we can walk him out between the two of us. He's tall but looks underweight. Pretend he's going for a walk to the restrooms," Rohan said. "Whatever we decide, we've got to do it soon, preferably before they decide to put him in a hospital gown. He'll look more conspicuous with his ass hanging out of a gown."

A loud beep sounded, followed by running footsteps. Ambar went to the doorway and glanced up and down the hall. "There seems to be a crisis in one of the other rooms. I think we should try to sneak him out while they're busy. There are visitors as well. Did you see a sign for the stairs? We should probably go down that way."

Rohan grimaced. "We're on the tenth floor."

"I'll make sure I tell our mystery man how you flexed your muscles," Ambar said with a grin. She turned back to the bed, her eyes widening. "He's awake."

"Who are you? Where am I?" His voice was low and husky, his eyes a beautiful shade that wasn't blue or green but a shade in between. He wrinkled his nose and sniffed in the same way Rohan had earlier, an expression of confusion racing across his face.

"Can you stand?" Rohan asked, trying not to react to the trace of panic in the blue-green eyes. He wanted to take the man in his arms and comfort him. "You're in a hospital. We need to get you out of here before we have a situation."

"Situation?"

Ambar exchanged a telling glance with Rohan. The male displayed either confusion or plain stupidity. Rohan hoped he had intelligence in there somewhere because they were risking discovery by helping him.

"Who are you?" He scented Rohan and let out a soft purr. Moving closer, he rubbed his head against Rohan's arm, curling into his warmth.

"We're friends," Ambar said. "Please, let us help you."

The male rubbed against Rohan again. "Good friends?"

Rohan knew Ambar was watching and would notice the goofy grin on his face if he didn't pull his act together. From the moment he'd scented the other man, his gut had jingled with nerves. He'd never experienced such a huge wave of lust for another man. The need to jump the stranger made him restless. He prowled to the door and stared down the corridor. The commotion continued in the other room, and he could hear someone in authority rattling out orders.

"What is wrong with you?" Ambar muttered with a trace of impatience. "We have to get out of here. *Now*."

Yep, she'd noticed. The urgency in Ambar's voice prompted him to shake off the weird compulsion to touch the stranger's mouth with his and rub all over him, marking the man with his scent.

"Let me help you stand." Rohan slung his arm around the man's shoulders, barely suppressing a shiver of awareness. With Ambar on the man's other side, they managed to get him upright.

Ambar heard footsteps heading in their direction. "Hurry, someone's coming."

A nurse entered the room, coming to an abrupt halt when she saw the mystery male standing between them. "What are you doing? He should be in bed."

"Don't like hospitals," the male said. "Taking me home."

"That's right," Rohan said smoothly, winking at the nurse.

Ambar released the male and took the nurse's arm after gesturing for her to come closer. "Sorry," she said.

"Why?" the nurse asked.

Ambar grabbed her and pressed down on her neck. Seconds later the nurse slumped against Ambar's chest, and she hauled her toward the hospital bed.

Rohan scowled at his sister as he removed everything attached to the man and hoped for the best. "What did you do that for? Is she okay?" His breath eased out when no alarms went off. He hesitated when it came to the drip, gave a sharp tug, and jerked it out of the back of the man's hand. It didn't bleed much, which was a relief. "Ambar?"

"Just unconscious." Ambar lifted the nurse onto the bed and pulled the covers over her so only the back of her head showed. "I don't like it any more than you do," she retorted when he frowned at the nurse. "But one of us had to do something. I guess you won't make fun of me for reading so much. Funny the stuff you learn in books."

"Let's go," Rohan said, shaking his head. His sister was amazing and going into business with her was one of the best decisions he'd made. He and Ambar were close. They both liked it that way, which made it imperative to talk to her about his sexual orientation soon.

"Never mind the stairs," Ambar said. "We'll take a chance with the elevator. If we act with confidence maybe no one will notice our departure."

Rohan didn't reply. He couldn't. The stranger's scent pervaded every breath he took, filling him with hope and sexual arousal. He concentrated on putting one foot in front of the other and prayed Ambar didn't notice his predicament. A hospital gown would have killed him. The tight black jeans were bad enough, leaving nothing to his imagination. The man had an arse he'd kill to touch.

Ambar darted to the bank of elevators and pressed the call button. They waited in tense silence, watching the indicator lights. A woman and two young children joined them, apprehension ratcheting up inside Rohan. A nurse walked past, her gaze scanning them. Her gaze halted on the stranger. She hesitated, then continued past to the reception desk.

The stranger leaned on him, breathing audibly. Rohan sensed the mother and children watching them and prayed the elevator would arrive soon. He didn't like it here, the fear of capture, the danger to them all rippling through his mind like a bad action movie sequence.

At last, the elevator arrived, the doors sliding open in a smooth whir. Ambar stepped inside the car and took possession of a corner. She stepped aside, allowing him and the stranger to maneuver behind her. She took up a position in front of them, reminding Rohan of a guard.

The stranger patted his butt, making Rohan jump. Okay, this weird attraction wasn't one-sided. Just as well Ambar couldn't see. Rohan took a deep breath and removed the male's hand, frowning at him. The low masculine chuckle in reply to his silent censure created a raft of goose bumps on Rohan's arms and legs. Rohan's scowl deepened and worry creased his forehead. They'd never make it out of here if the stranger created a scene.

The ride to the ground floor took ages, the elevator stopping on every level. The tension inside Rohan increased with every hospital staff member who joined them inside the elevator.

Finally the elevator stopped. Ambar took the stranger's other arm and they exited with confidence despite his wobbly gait.

"Wait!" a masculine voice shouted behind them.

Fear jumped inside Rohan, and he caught the flicker of panic on his sister's face. The stranger merely looked confused.

"Yes?" Rohan said, his tone not far from a snarl as he studied the hospital employee. He watched the man's face, ready to run if necessary.

"You dropped your wallet," the man said, extending his hand.

"Huh! My brother would lose his head if it wasn't attached to his shoulders," Ambar said with a laugh. She stepped forward to accept the wallet.

"Thanks," Rohan said with a jerk of his head. Damn, he wanted to get out of here. *Now.*

"You smell good," the stranger said, his warm breath tickling across Rohan's ear.

A spear of pleasure shot through Rohan, sinking to his groin. A teenager's giggle brought him back and reminded him of the danger. Aware his sister had heard as well, Rohan started for the exit, shouldering most of the stranger's weight.

When they'd almost reached the car, Ambar ran ahead to unlock it. She opened the rear door and stood aside to let him help the shifter inside.

Rohan sucked in a breath, ultra aware of the attraction simmering between him and the stranger. With his arm around the man's shoulders, he could feel the heat coming off his skin. Rohan's cock filled enough to worry him. He held his breath, trying to think of cold things, mindful of Ambar standing behind them.

This wasn't how he wanted her to discover his preference for males. He scowled again. A tiger shifter and one he didn't know. What were the chances?

Grunting, he manhandled the stranger into the rear of Ambar's car, wishing they'd kept his SUV instead of selling it. That would have been much easier than squeezing the man into Ambar's small car. They'd sold Ambar's car as well, and the new owner would take possession on the day they left for Middlemarch. Rohan couldn't wait to take delivery of the new SUV they'd ordered in Dunedin.

"I like you," the stranger whispered. "Wanna fuck?"

Hell! Rohan went stock-still, his heart pounding so loud he was sure Ambar would hear the thumpity-thump as it drummed against his ribs. And that wasn't all that was hard. His dick pressed against the fly of his jeans with an insistent pressure that made him want to rearrange himself for comfort. He cursed and attempted to move. The stranger gripped his shoulders and yanked him forward. Off balance, Rohan landed on top, both of them lying on the backseat. Seconds later the stranger kissed him on the mouth.

Rohan froze. *Pull away. Laugh it off. Blame the kiss on the stranger not being in his right mind.* All these thoughts flashed through Rohan's mind, yet he followed none of them. The warm touch of the male's lips moving beneath his held temptation, pushed his restraint. His cock bucked, and when the stranger moved against him, Rohan gave up his losing fight. Rohan kissed him back despite the fact Ambar was watching. Despite the fact they were still parked in the hospital car park and in danger.

When Rohan finally lifted his head, they were both breathing hard. They stared at each other, the stranger lifting his hand to caress Rohan's cheek.

"Is there something you want to tell me?" Ambar asked in a choked voice. "Huh, maybe when we get home," she added in a hurry. "Get into the car properly. *Now*. And keep down. Grab the blanket and pull it over him. I'll drive."

Adrenaline pumping at the urgency in Ambar's voice, Rohan crawled inside, lifted the stranger's legs clear of the door, grabbed the tartan blanket from the back and spread it over them both. The car door slammed behind them.

"Kiss me again," the stranger said in a loud voice.

"We are really going to talk when we get home," Ambar said tartly.

The car started, turning sharply and throwing them both off balance.

"Drive slow and smooth," Rohan ordered. "We don't want to attract attention."

"Shush. I need to concentrate."

Rohan shut up. A mistake because then he had time to appreciate his proximity to the stranger, take in his scent and feel the hardness of the man's erection pressing into his hip.

"Kiss—"

Rohan kissed him, telling himself it was a good way of shutting up the stranger. The first kiss had started off as a mashing of lips with no finesse. This one was different, as if the other man felt more alert. His tongue licked the seam of Rohan's lips, and he pressed the tip against the corner of Rohan's mouth. Immediately, Rohan envisaged penetration. A shot of pure lust converged in his gut, the reverberation ending in his balls. He gasped, more turned-on than he could ever remember, and he didn't even know the man's name. The thought drifted away when pitched against the touch of the man's lips, sucking and nibbling on the tendons of his neck.

"I like kissing you," the stranger said. "You make me hot. I can't wait to fuck you."

Rohan pulled away, breathing hard. He pressed his fingertips to the stranger's mouth, wanting him to quieten. Ambar didn't need to hear this stuff.

The stranger fell silent, and Rohan let his breath ease out in relief. Judging by the speed of the car, Ambar had left the parking area and was on the main road.

"Is anyone following?" he asked.

"I don't think so. I saw a couple of men run from the entrance. They were wearing uniforms, but I don't know if they were after us or not."

"Best to be sure," Rohan said.

"Yeah." A loud sigh sounded, and Rohan imagined Ambar had breathed hard enough to stir the lock of hair that sometimes fell over her forehead. "You'd better stay under the blanket and keep out of sight. If anyone is looking for us, a car with a driver and no passengers might throw them off."

A rough tongue dragged across his fingers, the abrasive sensation making him gasp. The stranger was going to kill him. Warm heat surrounded his fingers and the man sucked on them. Rohan swore.

"Do I want to know why you're cursing?" Humor lurked in Ambar's voice this time, and although Rohan worried about the talk he knew was coming once they reached the safety of their home, he thought it might not be as bad as he'd imagined. She sounded curious and intrigued rather than disgusted.

They'd become close during childhood, teaming up against their parents' strict child-raising methods. Rohan had loved his parents, and he knew Ambar had as well, but there was no disputing they'd lived in the dark ages, believing in traditional roles for men and women and arranged marriages. Both still single by sheer luck and many arguments, they were ready for a new chapter in their lives. Rohan made a mental note to make sure he canceled the marriage broker. Ambar was still on the books. He'd ring India later today to ensure they were both free to follow their own paths.

The stranger swiped his tongue up and down Rohan's finger and sucked again.

"Quit that," Rohan snapped, snatching his fingers free of the stranger's mouth when all he wanted was to sink into the pleasure. He wanted to rip off the stranger's T-shirt and run his hands over his chest. Rohan blinked and stopped his thoughts above belt level. No point sinking any farther into the gutter.

"Almost back to the store," Ambar said. "For once I've struck most of the lights green."

"Is the sky falling?" Rohan asked. The rest of New Zealand made jokes about the constant snarl-up on Auckland roads, and for good reason. The traffic was horrendous.

"Oh shoot. There are two customers waiting in front of the store."

"Okay, give me a few minutes to get this guy up to the flat and you can open up. I'll settle him and try to get some answers. His name."

"You're gonna owe me," Ambar snapped. "One of the customers is Brian Gibson. I swear if he tries to touch my arse again I'm gonna deck him using every ounce of my strength. I won't care about holes in the walls or his head or anything else. Do you hear me?"

"Shrew, they can probably hear you on the other side of the world," the stranger said.

The car braked so abruptly Rohan hit his head on the seat in front. The man grunted when his cock slammed into Rohan's hip.

"I hope that hurt," Ambar said sweetly. "Bro, you owe me." The driver's door opened and closed.

Rohan pushed aside the blanket and shoved off the stranger. His face flamed. Hell, his entire body shimmered with heat, and a blind man would notice his erection. Ambar wasn't sight-impaired.

The rear door opened, and Ambar scrutinized them. Thankfully she didn't comment on their appearance. "Do you need help?"

"Just get the door for us. I'll help him up the stairs to the flat. As soon as he's settled, I'll come to help you in the store. You have my permission to hit Brian if he gets out of hand."

"Pretty," the stranger said.

Rohan hid the surge of disappointment behind a stoic face. That would be right. Half the men he met had the hots for his sister. Why should this one be any different? Someone had drugged him and maybe worse. No wonder he had an addled head. The kiss meant nothing. Sighing, Rohan turned to find the man staring at him, not Ambar.

Ambar's eyes narrowed. She made a tiny noise at the back of her throat that could mean anything and stomped over to the door leading to their flat above the store. Her expression told Rohan their talk would come before the day ended. He climbed from the car and leaned back inside to grasp the other man.

"I can do it," the man said.

Rohan suppressed a smile at the snappy tone. It reminded him of a determined child, intent on testing his skills.

"Don't be long," Ambar called, disappearing inside.

Rohan watched the stranger, ready to grab him if he faltered. After long seconds, the man stood beside him. He wavered from side to side, resembling a sailor walking on land after a long sea voyage.

"How are you feeling?" Rohan asked. "What's your name? I'm Rohan Patel and that was my sister Ambar."

In the distance, he heard the roar of a lion, followed by the screech of primates. The familiar sounds, coming from the nearby Auckland Zoo, calmed the angst residing in his gut.

The stranger tensed, his head jerked and he turned to face the direction of the disturbance. The lion roared again.

"Easy," Rohan said. "It's the lions. The zoo isn't far from here." Not that Rohan blamed the man for his unease. Difficult not to feel anxiety, given the circumstances.

"Sister." A grin transformed the man's countenance as he turned his attention back on Rohan. "That's good to know. I thought you might have been married."

"No," Rohan said, holding back the surge of relief. "I wouldn't have kissed you if I was with anyone else." No sense getting ahead of himself. They knew nothing of this man, apart from his shifter status. They might go up in flames when they touched each other but that didn't mean they were compatible. "You didn't tell me your name."

"My name is..." The male trailed off, his brow furrowing in consternation. "My name is..." He wobbled and Rohan's arm shot out, slipping around his waist to steady him. "I don't know my name." A trace of panic coated his words, echoing in his stricken expression.

"It's all right," Rohan soothed. Another layer to the puzzle. Maybe he'd hit his head and that had something to do with his memory problems. Although when they'd kissed, Rohan had noticed the faint sickly sweetness

24

present when someone took drugs. Something else to check on... "Do you know where you come from? How you ended up in the hospital?"

The man's frown intensified. "I...I don't know. I can't remember anything."

They stepped inside. Rohan closed the door after them, turning the lock to make sure no one else could enter without a key.

"Don't worry." Rohan helped the man up the stairs, taking most of his weight by the time they reached Rohan's bedroom. He helped the man sit and bent to remove his dirty shoes. It took a bit for him to tug them off and he noticed two huge blisters on the man's heels. "Where did you get the clothes?"

The man shrugged. "I don't know."

"Stand and let me help you undress. Then you can have something to eat and a sleep."

"Not hungry," the man said.

"Okay." Rohan wished they were already in Middlemarch with the services of the doctor. He could have called on the services of the local shapeshifter doctor, but he only wanted to do that as a last resort because neither he nor Ambar liked the man's nosiness. They'd have to play it by ear and hope for the best. With only half his mind on the task, it took Rohan a while to notice the familiar scent. He froze when the smell registered and pressed his nose to the man's chest. He hadn't noticed it earlier because he'd been too busy kissing the stranger and while in the hospital they'd had one eye on the door the entire time in case medical staff turned up. He wrinkled his noise and sniffed again. Yeah, no doubt about it.

The zoo.

"I know that smell. You've been at the zoo." He took a closer look at the clothes and realized they didn't fit properly. The T-shirt swamped the man's chest while the faded black jeans barely buttoned. "Or maybe the clothes have been at the zoo."

"Rohan!" Ambar hollered.

"Can you undress yourself?"

"I'd rather you did it," the man said in a smoky voice.

Rohan's gaze shot to his face. The heat in the stranger's eyes sent blood roaring to his groin. The blood had scarcely drained after their car journey. Damn, he didn't need this now.

"Rohan!"

"I have to go. I'll be back as soon as I can. The bathroom is two doors down. Don't come down to the store because the locals gossip. We need to keep your presence a secret. Okay?" Rohan waited until the man nodded in acquiescence.

Rohan strode from his bedroom, fighting the urge to strip off his clothes and climb into bed with the stranger. At least the man's presence took one worry off his shoulders—when to tell Ambar about his sexual preference for males. If she hadn't guessed after the display in the car, she'd learn quickly enough.

He found the store empty when he stepped behind the counter. Outside Mrs. Rogers' ten-year-old twins tugged their bicycles from the special rack Rohan had installed for customer use.

"What's up?" He frowned when she switched on the radio, and he reached to turn it off. Another of his parents' ingrained rules. No music in the store during opening hours.

"Don't. I want to hear the news. Scott and Tom Rogers just informed me a tiger escaped from the zoo. Their mother rang their cell phone and told them to come straight home."

"Hell, do you think we have the tiger upstairs in our flat?"

"I don't know what to think," Ambar snapped. "That's why I want to listen to the news."

Ambar fiddled with the radio dial and the serious tones of a newsreader filled the store. "The tiger escaped over three hours ago and has not been sighted since. If you arrive home and find a tiger in your backyard, stay in your car and call the police."

Ambar switched off the radio when the strains of a pop song started. "What do you think?"

"He can't remember his name. He doesn't know where he came from or what happened."

"Do you think he's telling the truth?"

Rohan shrugged. "I don't know. All I know is he looks confused whenever he can't answer my questions. You're a good judge of character. See what you think when you talk to him. One thing I do know is he's been around the zoo. His clothes smell of the place. I missed it when we were in the hospital, but it could be a coincidence."

They stared at each other for a long moment.

"You think?"

"No, not really," Rohan said. "I think we have the tiger upstairs in my bedroom."

"Your bedroom?"

Shoot. "Yeah."

"I think that besides packing the last of our gear tonight we need to have a chat."

Rohan sighed and tried to avert his sister's thoughts. "Hell, I just remembered. I haven't contacted the marriage broker to cancel your listing."

Ambar scowled. "I'm perfectly capable of choosing my own partner. I don't know what Mum and Dad were thinking signing me up. And it's archaic for them to only accept cancellations from a male. Do *not* forget to ring India and cancel, Rohan." She turned away when the bell above the door tinkled to announce the arrival of a customer before whispering quickly, "You do that tonight, and afterward we'll discuss your love life." An impish grin filled her face. "That should be all kinds of interesting."

CHAPTER TWO

AT SIX, THEY CLOSED the shop. It was earlier than usual, but since they had two days before the new owners took over, he and Ambar had decided to shut early to organize the last of their packing before the move to Middlemarch.

Ambar started the cash up while Rohan went to check on the stranger. He found him sound asleep, his clothes tossed over the end of the bed. He lay on his back, the covers draped low on his waist, his easily discernable ribs highlighting his need of a few good meals. At least they could fix that. The man stirred, rolling to his side, and Rohan saw several old scars on his back. Rohan frowned, not liking where his mind went on seeing those scars. Had someone beaten him? The man flopped onto his back again. His breathing sounded normal and even, so Rohan ripped his gaze off the enticing sight and forced himself to leave the room.

Back downstairs, he restocked the laundry powder and cleaning material aisles, his mind on their guest and Middlemarch. What the hell were they going to do?

Ambar grabbed the money to take to the safe, pausing at his side. "What are we going to do, Rohan?"

"I've been thinking about that. The obvious solution would be to take him with us to Middlemarch."

"What if someone follows us? Or we take him to Middlemarch and he turns into a problem. We don't know him, but we'd be responsible."

Rohan pictured the male asleep in his bed and knew Ambar was right to preach caution despite his gut instinct and his yearning to keep the man with them. There was something about him that called to Rohan. He wanted to know him better. He wanted to care for him. A snort escaped. If that didn't beat all. A big strong tiger shifter like him turning soft. Nah, wouldn't happen. It was frustration, that's all.

"Rohan?"

"Sorry, just pondering our alternatives. We could leave him here, find somewhere safe for him to stay." He moved on to the canned-vegetable section.

"But what if he gets sick again?"

"Or I could contact Saber Mitchell in Middlemarch and tell him what's happened. He's on the Feline council and might give us advice."

"Yeah, that might work. There's a police car pulling up outside the store." Alarm shaded his sister's words.

"Don't panic. It might be nothing. Leave the talking to me."

"I really like it when you pull male rank and treat me like a defenseless woman," Ambar snapped sarcastically. "Our mother and father might have run their marriage like that, but don't think you can treat me the same way."

"I'm cancelling the arranged marriage contract, aren't I? They mightn't even want to talk to us," Rohan said. "Shush!"

One of the cops tapped on the door. Rohan placed the can of baked beans he held in his hands on the shelf and stood to answer the summons.

"You're shut earlier than usual," the cop said.

Rohan recognized him as a local who often dropped in to grab milk or the paper. "The new owners take over in a couple of days." He pointed to the sign in the window explaining the change in ownership and the reduced hours.

"Jeez, I hate moving," the cop said. "Rather you than me. We're doing a door-to-door asking about the tiger and making sure everyone knows what to do if they see it."

"I heard about the escape on the news," Ambar said, sashaying over to them.

Rohan hid his grin when the cop's gaze darted to her breasts and lingered. "I thought they would have captured it by now."

"That's the weird thing. No one's seen it. The tiger attacked the vet doing tests on it and escaped the surgery."

"Is the vet okay?" Rohan asked, exchanging a worried look with Ambar.

"So they say," the cop said. "If you see the tiger, ring the police station."

Ambar nodded. "We'll do that. Not many places for a tiger to hide around here, except the zoo. I presume the cops have searched the Western Springs reserve?"

"Yeah. We've had a few possible sightings but nothing has panned out. Not to worry. No doubt we'll get him soon." The cop waved and left. Rohan locked the door after him.

"Huh!" Ambar said. "If they've had sightings they're taking a long time to capture the tiger. I bet it's fevered imagination from excitable locals."

"We could always ring up and give them an anonymous tip," Rohan said. "Misdirect them."

"But we're not even sure our mystery man is the escaped tiger."

"His clothes smell of zoo. It would explain why no one has sighted the tiger since his escape and why our mystery man was so out of it. I bet they'd pumped him full of drugs."

"Makes sense," Ambar said. "I think you're right. We should ring Saber Mitchell. We both liked him when we did the video conference call to apply to move to Middlemarch. Besides, he told us to contact him if we had any questions."

They finished their work downstairs and went up to the flat together.

Ambar paused at the top of the stairs. "Do you want me to pour you a drink while you check on our guest?"

"Thanks."

Since their parents' death they'd started a new tradition—a drink before dinner where they discussed anything and everything. Their parents hadn't approved of alcohol either, and the ritual made them feel like rebellious teens.

Rohan joined Ambar in the small lounge. The room appeared stark and plain with only a single three-seater couch left. A stack of boxes piled against one wall, ready for collection by the removal company.

"He's still asleep. I've been thinking about Saber Mitchell. Maybe we shouldn't do anything and just take him with us."

"Because you have the hots for him." Ambar took a sip of her wine. "Are you gay?"

Rohan almost choked on his beer. Ambar didn't believe in tiptoeing around anything. He bit back a smile, knowing he was lucky she didn't sound judgmental. Her voice held curiosity but none of the distaste he'd feared. "Why would you think that?"

"You didn't run away in horror when the stranger said he wanted to fuck you. And I'm not blind. I know an erection when I see one."

"Ambar! Hell." There were limits to their closeness. They'd never talked about sex in such detail before. Fiery heat seeped into his cheeks, and he couldn't look his sister in the eye.

"I know you dated women but I never saw you kiss any of your dates," Ambar continued.

"Were you spying on me?" He didn't have to pretend exasperation. A man should have some privacy.

"At least you were allowed to date," his sister reminded him, and just like that his irritation dispersed. He'd had way more freedom than Ambar and he knew it. He checked his watch and mentally calculated the time in India. Not right yet. He'd have to make the phone call to cancel the marriage broker arrangement later.

"You didn't answer my question."

After their parents had died, they'd made a pact to be there for each other and to tell the truth. It was time he lived up to their deal.

"Yeah, I'm gay. That's part of why I wanted to go to Middlemarch. I know there are a few same-sex relationships down there. From what Saber told me there's a *ménage a trois* as well."

"I must have missed that part of the discussion." Ambar cocked her head, making her look like an inquisitive bird. "Why did he tell you that? It might put some shifters off moving to Middlemarch."

"You were too busy checking out the other Mitchell males to listen," Rohan said dryly. "I think he wanted to make a point about tolerance and different feline shifter species living together."

Ambar cocked her head to the other side, a mischievous smile twitching her lips. "You must admit the Mitchell males are babes. A pity most of them are mated." She paused to take a breath, her eyes shining with the memory of the Mitchells. "A threesome? Hmmm, how does that work? I understand the mechanics of two males together but in a threesome... What goes where?"

Rohan spluttered, set his bottle of beer aside and laughed aloud. "The woman in the threesome relationship is a lion. Maybe you should ask her because she's the...um...expert. How...what do you think? About me?"

Ambar reached across the gap between them and covered his hand with hers. "You're my brother and I love you. All I want is for you to be happy. I don't care who you decide to love or settle with as a partner as long as they treat you right."

Rohan's throat tightened and the words he wanted to say lodged behind the obstruction. He swallowed and managed to whisper, "Thanks."

"No problem. So back to the stranger. We take him with us and hope he doesn't cause any trouble? And don't bother checking with Saber Mitchell?"

"Yeah, I think so."

Ambar nodded. "The pair of you can see if you're compatible meanwhile."

"Funny, I never thought of that angle." Rohan smirked, unable to hide his fascination in the other man any longer.

"Just remember I'm an impressionable virgin," Ambar said. "Don't shock me too much, okay?"

"Deal."

They both laughed and finished their drinks before preparing dinner together.

Later that night, Rohan checked on the stranger and found him still asleep. Inside his room, he hesitated before retreating. Despite his yearning, he'd grab a couple of blankets and sleep in their parents' old room. Time enough for getting to know the other shifter when he was on the road to recovery. He checked his watch and went to the phone to cancel Ambar's contract with the marriage broker. Ten minutes later he hung up, glad to have the chore completed.

ROHAN WOKE ABRUPTLY, UNCERTAIN of what had yanked him from sleep. Then he became aware of his hard-on, the hand stroking his cock, the warm mouth sucking on the tip. He made a choked sound, his superior eyesight making out the stranger bent over his groin.

The stranger lifted his head and grinned. "Don't you like me doing that?"

"Hell yeah," Rohan blurted. "But you're not well. You should be in bed."

"I am in bed. I woke up a while ago and couldn't go back to sleep. I came to find you." He dipped his head and licked across the crown of Rohan's cock.

An embarrassing whimper escaped Rohan and the stranger chuckled.

"Good, huh?"

More than good. He hadn't had a chance to have sex with another male for too long to remember. With his parents throwing women at him and the subsequent upheaval after their death, his sex life had come last to other more important things.

"Yeah." There was nothing like the closeness and intimacy of being with a like-minded male.

"Has it been a while for you?"

Rohan laughed. "Obvious, huh?"

"You're trembling and you're really close," the stranger said.

"You don't have to do this."

"I want to." He glanced up at Rohan and winked. "I'm hoping you'll return the favor because I'm horny as hell."

"You're gay?"

"Don't like labels."

"How do you know?" Rohan retorted. "You don't even know your name."

"Kiran," the stranger said with triumph.

"Your memory is back?"

Kiran frowned. "No," he said finally. "All I know is my name. I can't remember a thing, other than hitting the man at the zoo. The ambulance and the hospital." He froze, horror skittering across his face. "They took blood at the hospital. I tried to stop them but I kept drifting off. My head felt stuffed with cotton wool when I first woke. Feels better after a sleep."

"Don't worry. No one knows you're here."

Kiran relaxed a fraction. "My memory should come back. Right?"

Rohan hoped so. He could only imagine how frustrating it must feel not knowing anything about the past. "You have an accent. It sounds as if you're from India, but your skin is lighter than mine. I'd say you have at least one English parent."

"I have an accent?"

"Yeah. That's good. It means you're a visitor. I wonder if you're staying at a hotel, although that wouldn't explain what you were doing at the zoo or how you came to be pumped full of drugs."

"No talk. Rather get back to what I was doing." He took Rohan's cock into his mouth and laved and sucked with real expertise, his eyes glinting with mischief as he peeked up at Rohan.

"Shit, you've done this before."

Kiran lifted his head briefly. "I think so." He took Rohan deeper, letting the flat of his tongue stroke along the delicate underside.

Rohan bucked his hips upward, driving his cock deeper into Kiran's throat. He shuddered, the pleasure building in his balls. They were so hard he thought they might implode. Damn, Kiran did this well. It was much better than jerking off in the shower. *Much better*.

Kiran increased his suction, using greedy noises that made Rohan glance at the bedroom door. Shut. He relaxed to enjoy the sensations racing through his body, the pounding of his heart, the pressure in his balls and the warmth of Kiran's mouth working his dick.

"Damn, that feels good," he said in a low voice, aware his sister was only a wall away.

Kiran used his hands on Rohan's lower shaft and ran a finger down his perineum, rubbing insistently across Rohan's puckered entrance. The gentle sawing motion, combined with Kiran's mouth, shoved Rohan into climax. Jets of semen blasted from his cock for long blissful moments, the tension leaching from his muscles.

With a final swipe of his tongue, Kiran lifted his head to grin at Rohan. "Great stress release, huh?"

"Yeah. Come up here."

When Kiran moved up the bed, Rohan embraced him, feeling the faint raised edges of the scars beneath his fingertips. A wiry and naked body slid next to his. "You're naked."

Kiran kissed his jaw. "Fortunate, isn't it?"

They exchanged a glance, the lack of light no barrier for the eyesight of tiger shifters.

Rohan grinned. "Convenient, but not so good if you'd gone to my sister's room by mistake."

"No problem there. I followed your scent." Of one accord, they kissed, taking it slow and easy. A gentle meeting of lips and a thrust of tongue. They kissed for a long time, building the pleasure between them, learning what each of them enjoyed.

When they pulled apart, they were both breathing hard. Rohan kissed across Kiran's jaw, the brush of stubble reminding him he kissed another male. He took playful nibbles, working his way down Kiran's neck. He reached the spot where feline shifters traditionally marked their mates, nipped and froze when Kiran groaned. His entire body shuddered, and an electric shock zapped down Rohan's spine, coming to rest in his balls.

Rohan jerked his mouth away in shock, a harsh breath ripping down his throat. "Sorry." His hand trembled. He wanted to say more but his mind refused to produce the words. *It couldn't be. They couldn't be mates.*

His parents had informed him and Ambar that true mates were a myth. Respect and marriage for mutual benefit worked better than allowing the heart to rule.

Emotions should never enter a marriage. Of course, if the Middlemarch felines mated, there was no reason why tigers shouldn't have the ability to do the same.

"That's never happened before." Kiran's brow wrinkled. "That I remember. Do it again."

Rohan didn't move. "I don't think I should. I had an urge to bite."

"Bite?"

"That would mean we were mates," Rohan said, uncertain of what to do or feel, given the circumstances.

"Mates? Is that good? It felt good," Kiran said. "I don't remember about mates."

"Maybe it will come back to you soon."

"What if my memory doesn't return?" Kiran demanded. "How do I learn who I am? Where I come from? What if I'm married?" He held up his hands in a stop motion when Rohan recoiled. "I don't feel married, but what do I know?"

Even though he didn't want to move, Rohan knew he had to. "There's no point worrying about it. You need to rest, give yourself time for the drugs or whatever is in your system to pass through."

"Would I want to bite you if I had someone?" Kieran asked.

"No, or so they say. My parents didn't believe in a true mate for every shifter, which is why my knowledge is limited." Relief rippled through Rohan when he realized Kiran spoke the truth. According to his scant knowledge, if Kiran had a mate they wouldn't feel this weird urge. And they both felt it. That was clear from their erections, the way they both trembled when they received a kiss at the base of their necks.

"Can we ask your parents? Where are they now?"

"They died in an accident. A truck didn't stop at a red light."

"I'm sorry."

Rohan sighed. "It's okay. Ambar and I miss them but we're doing all right. On the plus side they died before they could formalize marriage contracts for either of us."

"With a woman?"

Rohan laughed. "Yeah. I managed to scare most of them off by hinting at my preference for kinky sexual practices."

"Didn't your parents find out?"

"I was lucky, although I'm not sure how much longer I could have held off their determination."

Kiran brushed a kiss on his lips. "Lucky for me."

"But we don't know if you have someone in your life. I can't..." Rohan trailed off as the enormity of their problem came to him. "I can't have sex with you if you're married. I'm sorry but I believe in fidelity. I don't, won't cheat."

"What if I never regain my memory? What then?" The accent of India lay heavy in his words.

Rohan pulled away and moved toward the edge of the bed to put distance between them. He noticed his hand trembled and he tucked it between his knees. "I don't know."

A snort erupted from Kiran. "So you're going to walk away because I can't remember my past?"

Rohan swallowed, feeling the pull to the other man, wanting desperately to touch even though he shouldn't.

41

Before they stepped into any relationship, Rohan needed the truth. "I...I don't know what to do, but I hate the mystery."

"You couldn't have discovered this before I sucked you off?"

Rohan sprang off the bed and glared at Kiran. "You took me by surprise. What was I meant to do, waking up like that?" Rohan held up a hand to stop Kiran when he started to speak. He sighed. "Look, I'm sorry. This is happening fast. Honestly, I don't think you have a mate because of the strong physical tug between us. You don't have a mark. I didn't mean to imply you were cheating, but I am concerned about your lack of memory. I want to take things slow."

Kiran stood and glared back. "What am I meant to do?" He gestured at his erect cock.

Rohan was in Kiran's face before he'd realized he'd moved. He grabbed Kiran by the shoulders and shook him. "This is not my fault. I didn't come to you. You came to me."

"Frightened?"

Rohan scowled and tried not to breathe in Kiran's seductive scent. Even tinged with the faint smell of zoo he drew Rohan, captured his attention. A quick glance at Kiran's mouth was a mistake. The desire to draw the other man against his chest and grind their lips together gnawed at Rohan. He leaned closer before he could control the movement.

"Kiss me."

If Kiran had taunted him again, Rohan might have found the willpower to step away. Instead, the plea in Kiran's voice pushed past his restraint. With a soft groan, he covered Kiran's mouth with his and kissed him. It was sweet. It was tentative. It was everything he'd ever dreamed about when he considered being with a male lover. Their lips moved together before Rohan deepened the contact. He flicked his tongue across Kiran's upper lip. When Kiran opened his mouth, Rohan took advantage, sliding his tongue inside to stroke Kiran's, his soft palate and the contrasting hardness of his teeth.

He slipped his hands over Kiran's shoulders and down his back, coming to rest on Kiran's butt. Rohan swiveled his hips, brushing their straining cocks together.

Kiran's groan seemed loud in the bedroom, jerking Rohan to the present. He pushed away from Kiran, holding him at arm's length, chest rising and falling rapidly.

"I can't think straight when I touch you. All I can think about is fucking you," Rohan said in a harsh voice.

"And it doesn't seem to matter that I know nothing of my past?"

Rohan let out a harsh breath as the truth hit him. "No." Hell, what did that make him? Maybe if he learned more about the mating process. If he and Kiran felt this strong attraction, surely there couldn't be another person in Kiran's life? He swallowed, going with truth once again. "No, it doesn't matter. I want you."

Kiran reached out and stroked Rohan's face. "Good." The brush of fingers against stubble made a faint rasping sound when he repeated the caress.

"I don't...can we take things slow?" Rohan closed his eyes, inhaled and opened them again. "I want...I need to get to know you better."

Kiran nodded. "That's fair. I like the idea of learning you."

"Good. That's...ah...good." Rohan took a step back and dragged a hand through his hair. He sat on the edge of the bed because his legs trembled. Rohan heard rather than saw Kiran round the bed to stand beside him.

"Can I stay here with you for the rest of the night?"

Rohan stared at Kiran for a long moment before nodding. He didn't have the willpower to send him away.

CHAPTER THREE

KIRAN WOKE FEELING SAFE. In the unguarded moments before full consciousness, his mind drifted, memories flickering like a movie inside his head.

A man. Tall. Naked. He towered over Kiran, his cock erect, the head red and almost angry-looking...

Someone stirred next to him and the memories receded, escaping like mist until his mind became a blank canvas. Kiran turned his head and stared at the sleeping man beside him. A slow smile bloomed.

Rohan.

His gaze shifted, and he studied his surroundings. They weren't familiar. A sparse room with no pictures or personal items. Nothing to jog his memory. Kiran turned back to watch Rohan. His straight black hair stuck up and stubble shaded his jaw. His chest rose and fell with each breath, the sound of his breathing just short of a snore.

Kiran glanced down the man's body, visible because he'd kicked off the blankets. A body with no surplus fat. Strong. Fit. Kiran's breath started to come faster, the familiar surge of desire shooting through his body to pool in his groin. He remembered sucking Rohan off the previous night, recalled how he tasted, the noises Rohan made deep in his throat when he came.

Kiran also remembered his promise to take things slow between them. He wasn't sure he could keep his word.

"Morning."

The raspy voice made Kiran start. His gaze shot to Rohan's face. "Hi."

"I want to kiss you."

"I thought we were taking things slow. One day at a time." Kiran's mouth twisted as he said the words. Fool. He shouldn't have agreed with Rohan. He should have argued, made him see that they wouldn't have a chance of keeping their hands off each other. Raised his guilt about the one-sided nature of their loving because he hadn't come while Rohan had climaxed.

Rohan laughed, the husky sound making Kiran's cock jerk, the sensation almost painful. Damn, he wanted to touch Rohan. His fingers itched with the pent-up desire.

Rohan moved, propping his body weight on one arm. "Can you remember anything?"

"Only you."

"That's too bad." Rohan's golden eyes glowed with temptation.

Kiran didn't even bother to fight his natural inclinations. He sprang, letting instinct guide him. Evenly

46

matched in size, Rohan could have struggled, maybe even fought him off, but he didn't try to escape.

He relaxed and grinned up at Kiran. "What are you intending to do with me, now that you have me under your control?"

"I know what I want to do with you, but I promised to get become acquainted first." *Fine time to get a conscience.* Kiran ran the thought through his head again and wondered what it meant, what kind of person that made him. Frustratingly, it was the only hint of a memory he had. Maybe he needed to relax, try not to force his mind and to gather clues when they came to him.

"How about some old-fashioned petting?" Rohan asked, amusement simmering in his voice. "Do you think you can control yourself enough to handle that?"

Kiran went with honesty. "I'm pretty close to the edge."

"There's no point living without a bit of danger."

"Why have you changed your mind?" Kiran asked. "I don't understand you. Hell, I can't turn myself off and on like a switch."

The humor faded from Rohan's face. "You're right. It's not fair, and I'm not being honest. It's intense, ya know?"

Kiran understood without Rohan saying more. Intense was a good word for it—this thing between them. It scared Rohan. Hell, it scared him because deep in his gut Kiran sensed his past wasn't savory. What if he wasn't worthy? The people he lived with...they didn't mate...

The thought melted as soon as he tried to follow it deeper to a natural conclusion.

"What? What is it?"

47

"When we're talking I have flashes of thoughts. I try to grasp them and they fade. I end up with nothing. It's frustrating."

"You're pushing too hard. You need to relax."

Kiran's mouth curled into a wry grimace. "Easy for you to say." To emphasize his point, he rocked his hips. The head of his cock grazed Rohan's hip. The spike of pleasure made him hiss.

They reached for each other at the same time, mouths meeting with hungry abandon.

A sharp knock sounded on the bedroom door. It opened abruptly before either of them had a chance to spring apart.

Ambar burst into the bedroom. "Rohan, he's gone. Oh! Oops." She held her hands up to her eyes, spreading her fingers to peek through the gaps a few seconds later. "You know a sight like that might scar a virgin like me for life." She closed the gaps between her fingers, screening her eyes again.

"Next time you'll know to wait until I tell you to barge inside my bedroom," Rohan retorted.

"I'm here," Kiran added.

"I noticed. And I've seen rather more of you than I ever wanted. Can't you cover up or something?" Ambar peeked through her fingers. "Very nice even though you're a bit skinny."

Rohan grasped a blanket and flicked it over their lower bodies.

Kiran frowned. "I'm not skinny."

"You could do with a few extra meals," Rohan said. "I noticed earlier but got distracted."

Ambar snorted. "Easy to see what distracted you. Lucky I'm a sensible girl. All the revelations hitting lately could have scarred me for life. First, I learn my brother is gay then I find him in bed. Naked, I might add, with a man."

"Ambar, shush," Rohan muttered. "Go and make us some coffee."

Ambar folded her arms across her chest. "What did your last slave die of?"

"Disobedience," Kiran said. An unexpected shudder of horror ran down his spine. The sound of a whip cracked through his mind, the scent of blood. This time he shoved away the memory. He hated to remember this one. His breath eased out again only when the memory faded to obscurity like the others.

Brother and sister stared at him before glancing at each other.

"What?" he asked.

Rohan looked somber. "It didn't sound like you were joking."

"I...there was something, but I can't remember." Not the entire truth, but it was as much as he was prepared to give.

"I'll go and make coffee," Ambar said. "I'll expect you both out in the kitchen to collect it. Dressed," she added in a firm voice. "It's not good for me to see naked men."

"She says that now," Rohan said to Kiran. "I bet she changes her mind in the future."

"Hmm, maybe a Mitchell would make me change my mind," she said, flashing an impudent grin.

They waited for her to leave the bedroom and close the door before they moved.

"You want to take a rain check on the making out?" Rohan asked.

"Sure." Kiran rolled away from Rohan, his mind protesting the action. Rohan made him feel safe, and he didn't want to lose that feeling. He sat on the edge of the bed and wondered about clothes. He didn't think he had any.

"Ambar is right. You look as if you need special care." Rohan rounded the bed and sat beside him. He ran his fingers over Kiran's back, hesitating even though he wanted to ask questions.

"What is it?" Kiran asked, absorbing the warmth from Rohan at his side.

"You have scars on your back." He ran his finger over them, and Kiran shuddered. They didn't hurt. It was Rohan's touch that brought the self-awareness.

"I don't recall the scars," he said, trying to peer over his shoulder.

"They're slightly raised."

"I don't remember." This time a snap sounded in Kiran's voice.

"We need to be patient. You'll get your memory back."

Kiran wished he had the same confidence. Once again he had the uneasy feeling he'd be better off not knowing about his past and his personal details. The thought of the past frightened him.

Rohan stood and grabbed a pair of jeans off the back of a chair in the corner of the room. He stepped into them, did up the zipper but didn't fasten the button at the top. "I'll grab you some of my clothes to wear. Be right back."

Rohan strode to his bedroom, deep in thought. He'd noticed the pain and anguish on Kiran's face. The man was confused. Hell, who wouldn't be, given the circumstances?

In his room he grabbed a T-shirt and a pair of sweats. Kiran would have to stay up here in the flat so he wouldn't need anything dressy.

One more day to go before they moved. He couldn't wait. The move to Middlemarch would bring new possibilities for all of them.

MIDDLEMARCH, TWO DAYS LATER

"I hate moving," Ambar said, stretching her arms above her head and settling on the deck of their new residence. It was an old wooden bungalow, single-level with a deck out the back that overlooked an overgrown garden. Their shop was two streets away on the main Middlemarch road. "The garden needs weeding. Someone should rescue those purple flowers."

"Pansies," Rohan said, studying the garden. "We'll get to it. We've barely arrived."

"I'm never moving again," Ambar said.

Kiran grinned and tugged on her long black braid. "What about when you mate? I'm sure there will be males in Middlemarch who have brains enough to appreciate your beauty." He felt as if he'd known brother and sister for years and was glad they'd invited him to Middlemarch with them.

Rohan snorted and cocked an eyebrow at him. "Don't lay it on too thick. My sister has brains as well as beauty." He handed Kiran a can of beer and Ambar a glass of wine.

Ambar took a sip of her wine before she spoke. "Yeah. I'm not stupid. You'd like me to start going out with someone to give you some alone time. You want to have wild monkey sex without worrying about me walking in on you or overhearing things an innocent virgin shouldn't hear."

"Ambar!"

Kiran's lips twitched while Rohan glared at his sister.

"What? It's true. I'm starting to feel like a third wheel the way you two make goo-goo eyes at each other all the time."

"We do not make goo-goo eyes," Rohan said, his eyes flashing with indignation.

Kiran hid his amusement while he listened to brother and sister quarrel. There was teasing and a lot of love beneath the bickering. It brought out envy in him, not that they made him feel like an outsider. They included him, accepting him into their small family without a quibble.

He wondered if they'd feel the same way once his memory returned.

"You can't see yourselves," Ambar retorted.

"You wait until a poor unsuspecting male asks you out. Kiran and I are going to give you a hard time," Rohan said. "See how you like it."

"Yep, count on it." Kiran grinned, leaning back against a pillar and breathing deep. The scent of the country filled his lungs, the air fresh without the tinge of motor vehicles. Instead he smelled flowers, cut grass and the scent of the beef stew he'd help Ambar cook earlier. The sounds were different too. Birds and animals. Laughter. Bicycle bells and farm tractors. A man could feel content here—even one suffering from amnesia.

"We're not sleeping together," Rohan added.

"But you can't keep your hands off each other," Ambar said, wrinkling her nose. "It's enough to make me wary about entering a room without peeking around the corner first."

Kiran glanced from Ambar to Rohan and found the other man watching him. Their gazes caught and held and it was like an electrical charge jolting his body. Despite the temptation, they'd confined themselves to kissing and touching rather than going for full sexual intercourse. He wasn't sure, but he didn't think he'd had a relationship like this before. Right now he wanted to touch Rohan. Craved it. He suspected it wouldn't be much longer before one of them broke.

Rohan ignored his sister. "Don't listen to her."

"Tomorrow is opening day," Kiran said. "Are you looking forward to it?"

"Ooh, good change of subject. Yeah. I can't wait to meet the locals." Ambar set her glass down and tipped back her head to enjoy the last of the day's sun. "Are we sure we should close at six every day?"

"I still think it's a good idea," Rohan said. "The move to Middlemarch is a lifestyle change more than anything. Neither of us wants to work the hours our parents did."

"You just want to have a life," Ambar teased, winking at Kiran. "I can see I'm going to have to make friends fast. I can't help having good hearing, you know. You guys will have to remember that."

"You're not going to guilt us out of this relationship, Ambar."

Kiran glanced from brother to sister again and thanked the stars they'd found him, that they'd cared enough to save him when he'd fallen into human clutches. The people he knew weren't like that— He broke the thought off when he realized he'd seized a memory but it slipped away like a dust mote. Sighing, he tuned back into the conversation. He'd think about that snippet later when he was alone.

Ambar's smooth brow puckered with her frown. "I'm not trying to do that. Rohan, really. I'm teasing. I'm glad you've found someone you like and felt you could tell me the truth. I don't mind that you're gay. It explains so many things."

Rohan turned to Kiran. "Remind me to give Ambar my headphones so she can listen to music instead of us."

Ambar winked at Kiran. "You'd better download noisy music for me. Something that thunders rather than rocks."

"Hello? Is anyone there?" a feminine voice called.

"That sounds like Emily Mitchell," Ambar whispered. "I met her earlier at the café. She's lovely. Out here!" she called, standing to greet their first visitor.

Emily Mitchell appeared around the corner of their house. "Hi, I hope I'm not interrupting," she said. "I wanted to know if you'd like to come for dinner tomorrow night. I thought we'd have a barbeque, something fairly informal. Some of the family will be there and a few of our friends."

"We'd love to," Ambar said, speaking for them all. "Emily, this is my brother Rohan and our friend Kiran."

"Pleased to meet you," Emily said with a smile, her hand resting on her pregnant belly. The last of the sun picked up the golden highlights in her hair.

Kiran found himself smiling back, liking the brown-haired woman instinctively. Somehow, he didn't think it was a normal reaction for him, but something about Emily's open smile and the warmth in her brown eyes told him she meant it. She really was pleased to meet them.

"Should we bring anything?" Rohan asked. "And would you like to have a drink with us? We have juice or tea."

"Thanks, maybe another time. I'm on my way home and Saber worries if I'm late." She paused to grin, her face lit up with love. "I'm fine in the food department. Why don't you bring a bottle of wine or whatever you'd like to drink?"

A cell phone rang and she pulled a rueful face. "Excuse me. I bet that's Saber. He's such a worrywart lately."

Kiran let his eyes close and savored the peace, the scents again. He heard movement and seconds later someone squeezed his hand. He opened his eyes and smiled at Rohan, committing the feelings, the moment to his memory. He might not remember his past, but he could make new memories.

"Saber," Emily said. "I'm fine. No, I'm with Rohan and Ambar Patel. I just stopped by to invite them to dinner tomorrow." She paused to laugh and Kiran heard a masculine voice but not the words. "Really. I'm fine. Just running a little late. I'm on my way home now." She hung up and with a grin at the phone, replaced it in her pocket. "I'd better go. I know tomorrow is your opening day, but come as soon as you close." After giving them directions, she hurried away.

"I like her," Ambar said. "I met her sisters-in-law today at the café as well. They both seem nice."

They lingered over their drinks before having a quick meal and heading back to the store to do some last-minute shelf stacking and preparation for the following morning.

Two hours later they returned to their new home. Kiran said good night to Ambar before turning to Rohan. He wished they could share a room, although he was enjoying the slow getting to know each other, the languid make-out sessions that made him so hot he wanted to pounce. He knew the touches, the kisses made Rohan just as hot and desperate. Several times during the day he'd sensed someone watching him and glanced up to meet Rohan's heated stare. It was a courtship, he thought, testing the word for size. Yeah, an old-fashioned wooing, and despite his impatience, he was enjoying every moment of it.

"Good night," he said.

Rohan moved closer. "It's getting harder and harder not to drag you into my bed."

"That's a bad thing?"

"You still don't know where you come from, who you are."

"I could have done something terrible." Kiran shuddered and stepped right into Rohan's arms, hiding his face against the other man's shoulder.

He didn't want to know. The past scared him. Every time he drifted to sleep, he had nightmares. They were becoming worse, more graphic, and he'd discovered he dreamed in color. Bright red swathes of blood decorated most of his dreams. He'd wake trembling, his body covered with clammy sweat, his heart racing. So far he'd kept the nightmares concealed from Rohan and Ambar but, with their graphic nature, he worried it was only a matter of time before he woke screaming. The idea of going to sleep worried him because he had no control. The dreams weren't even the same. They varied from night to night.

"Earth to Kiran."

"Huh?" He lifted his head and pushed back to arm's length.

Rohan laughed, his eyes sparkling with happiness. Kiran loved that look, would remember it to his dying day. He hoped he never did anything to drive the joy from Rohan's face.

"I said you looked tired."

"New place," Kiran said, shoving aside the anxiety even though the other man's concern made him warm inside. "Kiss me goodnight."

"With pleasure." Rohan drew him closer and their lips met.

As always, the kiss claimed Kiran's attention and drove away the blackness hovering out of reach. Their lips met, parted and met again. Rohan's familiar taste burst over him. His cock filled, but he ignored the bittersweet pain and concentrated on the kiss instead, the intimate twirl of tongues and the blooming pleasure. He sank into the kiss and wrung every emotion he could from the contact with Rohan. When they finally parted, they were both breathing hard.

For a long moment they stared at each other.

"Good night," Rohan said.

"Yeah." Kiran dragged a hand through his hair and forced a smile. "See you in the morning."

Kiran entered his small bedroom and prepared for bed. After brushing his teeth, he stripped off his clothes and crawled between the sheets naked, praying for a night of dreamless sleep.

It didn't happen.

Like a vicious storm, the dreams rained down on him. Kiran drifted above the scene, feeling like a ghost because, weirdly, he was also in the scene, secured to the foot of the large four-poster.

Naked, he wore a thick black leather collar around his neck, affixed to a chain. Every time he moved, the chain rattled. The heat from his back, hot stripes from the whip, radiated outward from his shoulder, a badge of his master's favor. The bloody things ached and itched like crazy, but not enough to take his mind off chaos created by the drugs in his system. His shaft strained upward, painfully hard. His muscles tensed at the vicious throb while his balls were one relentless ache.

The need to stroke his cock, to relieve the discomfort pulsed through him.

He knew better.

His master would beat him if he walked into the room and found him with a flaccid cock. A bead of pre-cum formed on the tip. He shifted position, trying to ignore the sensual pain in his body. But like a nagging tooth, his erection throbbed and taunted him.

One quick stroke.

It couldn't hurt.

He shifted his weight again to find a comfortable spot. For a few seconds his mind battled between the pain in his muscles and the ache in his groin.

His dick won.

With a quick glance at the door, he stroked his cock, groaning softly at the acute pleasure. Impatient with human frailties, his master had laced his water or food with tablets again to make sure his cock remained full. Ready. Kiran couldn't resist another furtive stroke. The chains holding him captive rattled and he froze.

The door sprang open and his master strode into the chamber. Two young men and a woman followed him, their heads lowered in respect, their naked bodies gleaming with fragrant oils.

Kiran almost felt sorry for them. Almost. They were the latest of the disposable servants the master collected from all parts of the world for his decadent games. If they failed to please him, they disappeared. Kiran didn't ask where they went—he didn't allow himself to care.

It was better that way.

At the master's palatial house only the fittest survived.

"I saw you pleasuring yourself, slave." The master referred to them all as "slave". "Don't deny it because I saw you on the cameras."

Kiran swallowed, knowing in the master's eyes he'd earned a punishment. It didn't matter that the drugs in his system were causing him pain, that he was so desperate he thought he might fuck anything to gain some relief. He hung his head, knowing better than to meet the master's gaze. "I'm sorry," he whispered.

"You might be repentant, but the problem remains. You disobeyed an order."

The master's uncompromising tone brought a slash of fear. His stomach twisted into a painful knot while he waited to hear the details of his punishment.

"Stand!"

Kiran pushed to his feet, biting his bottom lip to stem the cry of pain bubbling deep in his throat. Pins and needles attacked his lower limbs and he stumbled, the chains binding him rattling with a musical sound.

"Help him." The words were like a lash, the three silent slaves springing to action. They helped him stand and returned to their position behind the master. "Choose one," the master said, his tone bored and disinterested.

Kiran knew better because he'd seen the flash of excitement in the master's dark eyes. Taking a deep breath, he glanced at the three and picked the nearest male. He didn't choose him for a particular reason. Kiran chose because the master had ordered it so.

"Step forward." Another lash-like order.

The slave stepped to the indicated position with alacrity, his head remaining dipped in quiet respect.

The master drew a gun from beneath his embroidered tunic and shot the slave. The man fell to the ground, instantly dead. Blood poured from his chest and pooled beneath him. It happened so quickly Kiran scarcely had time to blink.

A squeak of terror escaped the woman. Kiran wanted to warn her not to make a sound or draw attention to herself but couldn't. The master didn't tolerate speech. As degrading as this position was, he didn't want to die. He dreamed of the day he could escape, make his own choices. He dreamed of freedom and running through a forest, swimming in a lake, the wind on his face.

The thought of freedom...it was the only thing that kept him alive.

That and the fact the master had taken a liking to him. Kiran had no idea why. It was true his looks were pleasing and attracted attention, but he came from a poor family. His education was patchy until he'd arrived at the master's house. He'd attended classes with the other children and continued to read and watch television to extend his knowledge. Sometimes the master talked instead of playing games. He liked his slaves to have an opinion at these times. At other times they were to remain silent and fuck...

The master retrieved a key from under his tunic and unlocked the padlock holding his collar in place. Kiran had wondered how to gain possession of the key. So far he hadn't thought of a way to take it without the master's knowledge.

"Turn so I can see your body from behind. Good. Turn back to the front." He tapped the head of Kiran's cock with a forefinger. It hurt in a good way. Another bead of pre-cum welled from his slit. "Very good, slave. Get some lube." He ignored the body lying on the floor, stepping over it casually. "Call the guards to remove the body."

The praise was rare and confused him. Kiran opened a sandalwood drawer, the fragrant scent of the wood starting his stomach churning. The master liked to wear the scent and Kiran loathed it because it meant the man had prepared for sex. He didn't think he'd ever manage to smell sandalwood without wanting to vomit. Taking one of the bottles of lube from the drawer, he set it by the bed. Cool air from a partially open window brushed over his skin. A shiver racked his body at the delicate caress, awareness pulsing at his groin until he felt as if he'd burst. He couldn't last much longer.

"On your hands and knees." The master gestured to the bed with its billowing white silk curtains and luxurious covers in vibrant red and white. A large bed made by skilled local tradesmen to sleep six, it bore a carved headboard depicting the gods and goddesses in sexual positions from the Kama Sutra.

Kiran walked to the bed, the sway of his cock making his heart pound with contrasting pain and pleasure.

"You. Prepare him. I want him clean and ready to receive me." He paused and Kiran caught him spearing a speculative glance at the woman. "Slave. You." He indicated the woman. "I will fuck you too. Get on the bed."

The master strolled over to a small table and took a seat, pouring himself some tea into a delicate china cup. He stared out at the garden, ignoring his slaves and the guards who removed the body and swiftly mopped the puddle of blood.

The woman's limbs trembled noticeably, her tear-filled eyes widening in fear. Kiran wanted to tell her to hurry, that the master was capable of shooting them all. He tried to tell her with his eyes, tried to reassure and coax her to speed with one telling look. Luckily, she seemed to understand and slipped on the bed beside him. Using careful stealth, Kiran eased his hand over the covers until his finger touched her hand. The contact seemed to calm her. Her breasts heaved when she inhaled.

"Lie on your back," the master ordered the woman. "Slave, I want my cock to slide into her cunt. When I pull out, I want to see her juices coating my cock. Make her ready for me first while I take tea. Then I will fuck him. Place a plug in him to keep him stretched. He is always a good fuck."

The slave prepared the woman, a combination of strokes and delicate licks of her labia and clit preparing her for sex. The woman remained so tense Kiran feared for her, her juices failing to flow. When the male slave shot him a helpless look, he jerked his head toward the lube. The male took his meaning and retrieved the bottle. Soon, the female prepared, he moved behind Kiran.

Kiran huffed an ironic sigh. Arousal wasn't a problem for him, even if his head wasn't with the program. For him the problem would be holding back.

The male slave's fingers fluttered over his hole, tentative and teasing. Kiran let out a harsh exhalation, gritting his teeth and fighting the need to move into the stroke. "Shove the plug in me," Kiran muttered with a cautious gaze at the master.

The slave chose a plug from the drawer and pushed it into him. With the plug fully seated, the burning sting in his channel grabbed his focus instead of the gnawing ache in his balls. He hung his head, attempting to breathe through the pain and waited, trying to reach the place inside his head where nothing mattered. The empty place where he hid from the truth of what his life had become.

He was a rich man's slave, a prisoner whose life depended on his sexual skills.

He was a whore.

The master slurped the last of his tea and set his china cup on its matching saucer with a clink. He stood, his muscular body moving with grace as he disrobed. He handed the jacket and trousers of his designer suit to the male slave who hung them to prevent creasing. The rest of his clothes went into the laundry hamper, his gleaming black shoes placed at the foot of the bed.

He strode to the bed and walked around from one side to the other, studying them like animals in a zoo. "Very good," he pronounced. "Spread your legs. Both of you. Ah yes. I have changed my mind. You, woman, may go. Keep your body ready. I may desire you later. Take her to the slave quarters. Let the guards help her."

Kiran swallowed and strove to keep his face passive. Once the guards got their hands on a slave, they were one step away from death. It was a game to the master.

The two slaves left, leaving Kiran alone with the master.

"Ah, how I have needed you. It has been torture staying away when all I wanted was to bathe my cock in your heat." He grasped the plug and pulled it out. Kiran's entire body shuddered when the twist of the plug grazed his gland. His muscles tensed and he scarcely breathed with the effort it took to hold back.

The master slid beneath him and took his cock into his mouth. It was both relief and torture. The smooth lap of the master's tongue made him groan. He bit his bottom lip, attempting to stem further noise.

"You may react," the master said, his voice gentle. Caring even.

Kiran stilled in confusion until the master sucked on the sensitive head of his cock. A pained and urgent groan escaped him this time and he didn't bother trying to cover his reaction. The tendons of his neck strained, his hips thrusting forward and driving his cock deeper into the master's mouth. The master didn't rebuke him, merely sucked harder.

Encouragement?

The master confused him. He seemed to take genuine pleasure from the sexual act, giving as well as receiving gratification.

Then Kiran ceased to think about the complexities of the master. He could no longer hold back. Orgasm crashed over him in painful waves, the contractions going on for long minutes. Finally the spasms ceased, but the relief was fleeting, his shaft still hard and erect because of the drugs.

The master released his cock and licked his lips, smiling.

"I require a condom, slave. I want you to put it on me and lie on your back."

Kiran cast him a surprised glance. Another departure from normal. Normally the slaves were a convenient hole for sexual relief.

Kiran followed the instructions and waited on the bed with his legs spread, open for the master to take his pleasure.

The master smiled and moved between his legs. Instead of taking as was his normal behavior, he touched, running his finger over Kiran's straining erection. He brushed a kiss over one inner thigh, scraped his teeth over the same area then sucked the tender flesh. Pain. Pleasure. They warred with one another while Kiran struggled to make sense of the situation.

"You make me hunger," the master said. "You bring joy and soothe the anger inside me."

Confusion filled him. What did the master mean?

The master laughed, a genuine sound that made Kiran's eyes widen. "You look surprised, but even my family have remarked upon my recent even temper."

With purpose he shifted and lined his cock up with Kiran's entrance. He pushed forward, the head of his cock forging through the resistance until he filled Kiran. Kiran tried to hold himself apart, tried not to enjoy the master's possession, but the fires of lust rampaged his body. His body arched into each stroke, and when the master leaned down to kiss him for the first time, he moaned his pleasure at the unheralded intimacy.

The pleasure grew with each stroke, flinging him into such rapture he didn't think he'd ever escape...

Kiran jerked awake, fear pounding through him while his cock pulsed with hunger. Sweat covered his body, and he picked up the corner of the cotton sheet to wipe his face. Before the thought even formed, he found himself standing at the door of Rohan's room. He opened the door, slid inside, and shut it firmly after him.

"Kiran?"

"I...can I sleep in your bed?" He hated the need in his voice but couldn't shake the residual fear chasing in circles through his mind.

"Sure," Rohan said. "You okay?"

"Dreams." Kiran crawled into the bed, edging close to Rohan and seeking his warmth despite the evening humidity.

"Do you want to talk about it?"

"I was a prisoner."

"A prisoner?" Rohan drew Kiran against his chest and wrapped an arm around his waist. Some of the tension eased from Kiran's muscles. "Do you think it was a dream or your memories?"

"I don't know." Kiran swallowed, feeling tears well at his eyes. "I hope it was just a dream because people died." With stumbling words, Kiran recounted his dream, the horror of the slave's blood sending renewed shudders through him. "It must be a dream, right?"

"I don't know," Rohan said. "It could be a mixture of truth and fiction. It could be your mind struggling to recall the past. Why don't we visit the doctor tomorrow? See what he makes of the dreams."

"You'd come with me?"

"Hell, yeah." A flash of white teeth and a tightening of Rohan's arms reassured Kiran. "I'm not letting any of those Middlemarch men or women get any ideas about you. Not when I've just found you," Rohan said.

"Yeah?"

"Yeah. You wanna fool around, or do you want to sleep?"

Fresh on the heels of the dream the last thing Kiran wanted was to think about sex despite the nagging ache in his balls. But he also needed a fresh image to overlay the one burned into his mind. "Can we do both?"

"Ah, the perfect answer."

"Good. Yeah, let me feel your cock rub against mine. Get some friction going."

Rohan rocked his pelvis and brought their erections into contact.

The air hissed from Kiran's mouth, the electric sensation of the curving glans sliding against Rohan, claiming his attention. Blindly, he sought Rohan's mouth. Their lips met in a collision, both moving their hips in an urgent tempo. Need for reassurance flared into incredible pleasure, contentment at Rohan's touch. Rohan's presence soothed the panic caused by the dream.

"Damn, that feels good. Your cock against mine," Rohan said.

Kiran grunted, jerking his hips, sliding their shafts together. His stomach hollowed, his breathing going shallow. Heat and pressure galloped through him, growing big and bright until he exploded into orgasm, the spasms going on for long moments. He was vaguely aware of Rohan coming, spurts of semen painting his stomach.

Gradually their breathing slowed, and they took the time for a leisurely kiss, a meeting of mouths and minds.

Kiran tried to show Rohan without words how much his embrace anchored him, how much he appreciated his concern and how much he wanted to stay in the home he'd found with the Patel brother and sister. He'd like nothing better.

Chapter Four

Rohan told Ambar about Kiran's nightmare while Kiran was in the shower.

"You should take him to see Gavin Finley today. He should have a proper checkup anyway, especially if you're gonna bump dangly parts. We don't know if he still has drugs in his system or something worse."

Rohan glanced toward the bathroom, noting the water had shut off. "I don't like leaving you on your own during our opening day." He ignored his sister's precocious remark about sex to concentrate on the main message. A checkup for Kiran.

"This is important," Ambar said. "Especially if you intend to keep him, and don't tell me you haven't thought about it. I'm not blind. I can see how it is between the two of you."

"You don't keep people."

Ambar waved her hand in an airy motion. "A figure of speech. You know what I mean."

"Are you sure you can cope on your own?"

"It's not as if you're going to take all day. Even if he does tests, it shouldn't take longer than an hour. Besides, I can call you if I run into problems. Here, pour some coffee." Ambar handed him three mugs and acted as though they'd settled everything.

Rohan hid a grin and followed her orders. His sister had bloomed recently, and it made him realize how smothered she must have felt with their parents. As a son, he'd had a lot more freedom, and he'd felt choked by their strict upbringing. Ambar must have felt much worse. While he missed his father and mother and knew Ambar did too, the independence was a real bonus. She deserved to enjoy their freedom.

Ambar walked over to the phone and rang a number. "Hello. Yes, I'd like to make an appointment. Is there a free slot this morning? This afternoon? Three? That will be fine. The appointment is for a friend. His name is Kiran. Okay. Thanks." She hung up and beamed. "There. All done. I'm sure it will be busier this morning. Things will settle down by the time you and Kiran need to leave for your appointment."

"How did you know the number?"

"I figured Kiran should go to the doctor and looked it up earlier," Ambar said.

Kiran walked into the kitchen, smelling of soap and man. Rohan's nostrils twitched and he stilled, inhaling his scent deep into his lungs.

"You have an appointment at the doctor's at three," Ambar said.

"I'm not going on my own," Kiran said, his voice flat. He looked trapped and searched the exits from the room as if he might make a run for it.

"No, I'm going with you," Rohan said. "Hopefully it won't take long. Ambar and I would both feel happier if we knew you were okay."

"Because you're worried I might hurt you? Spread a disease or something?"

Ambar shunted Kiran toward a seat and plucked one of the mugs of coffee Rohan had poured off the counter. She placed it in front of him. "Don't be silly," she said. "We both feel a bit guilty about not insisting you see someone when we were in Auckland. We want to ease our consciences and make sure we haven't caused you any harm."

Rohan held his breath, only letting it ease out when Kiran's shoulders lost their tension. Silently, he blessed his sister's quick thinking. Kiran needed to feel he mattered rather than thinking he was a burden.

"Besides," he added with a wink at Ambar. "If we intend to keep working you as hard as we have during the last few days we want to make sure you're healthy. We don't want our slave labor to croak." He could have kicked himself when he used the word slave, but Kiran didn't react, sipping his coffee instead.

Ambar sent him a chiding look.

"What's for breakfast?" Rohan asked.

"Scrambled eggs and toast," Ambar said. "And you needn't think I'm going to do all the cooking. One or both of you can cook tomorrow."

"I don't know if I can cook," Kiran pointed out. "I might have helped with the stew last night but nothing was familiar."

"I suspect we're about to learn the extent of your cooking skills," Rohan said cheerfully. "If I have to cook so do you."

Ambar served the scrambled eggs and handed plates to both men before joining them at the table.

An hour later they opened their new business to the public. Business was brisk from the moment the front door opened.

"What's with all the single men?" Kiran asked in an undertone.

Rohan watched a pair of males around his age scope out Ambar while dropping groceries into a shopping basket. "They're checking out the new woman in town."

"As long as they're not checking out the new male," Kiran said, moving closer to Rohan and growling under his breath.

"Not much chance of that," Rohan said. "I'm only interested in one male."

"Even though I don't know anything about my past?"

Rohan slid his hand around Kiran's shoulders. "I know all I need to know." Rohan's fingers caressed Kiran's butt and gave him a sly pinch. "Stop worrying."

Kiran liked Gavin Finley straightaway. The feline doctor was calm and gave off an air of competence. He gave him a thorough physical and took blood tests.

Kiran put his shirt back on and sat beside Rohan. "I've been having dreams."

"More like nightmares," Rohan added.

"And you can't remember anything about your past?" Gavin asked, tapping a pen on top of the small desk he sat behind. He peered at the screen of his laptop and added a note.

"No."

"Do the dreams make sense or are they disjointed fragments?"

Kiran tensed, thinking about the events in his dream. "They're more like scenes." He barely suppressed a shudder of horror when he recalled the blood and the master's uncaring attitude.

"And you say he collapsed?"

Rohan nodded. "My sister saw him collapse and realized he was a shifter like us. We sprung him from the hospital and suspect someone pumped him full of drugs."

"I'll know more once I check your bloodwork. The dreams could be your mind's way of helping you remember. It might help to keep a dream journal. Write down as many details as you can before you forget them."

"I don't want to be the man I am in the dreams," Kiran blurted. His impassioned words hung in the air between the three men, and embarrassment filled him. He hated the helpless feeling, the worry that he might bring danger to his new friends. The master—the man in his dreams—was a monster. Although he seemed to treat Kiran well, he cared nothing for the other slaves. Kiran sensed the master wasn't a man who liked opposition, and if he were real, all hell would break loose if he tried to recover his favorite slave.

Swallowing the wave of panic, he risked a glance at the doctor and put his greatest fear into words. "What if I'm dangerous? Or the people in my dreams are real and they're dangerous?"

Fleeting sympathy rippled across Gavin's face. "The not knowing must be difficult. Have you spoken with Saber Mitchell?"

"No, but we're going to a barbecue at the Mitchells' house tonight," Rohan answered for him. "We intended to talk to him anyway."

"Good, depending on what Saber thinks, you might also like to talk to the cops. They're both human but have shifter mates. Charlie McKenzie, one of my mates, is a cop."

"You have two mates?" Kiran asked.

"Yeah. Charlie and Leticia." Gavin's features softened and it was easy to see the love in his green eyes. "We're going to the barbecue tonight so you'll meet them there."

"We're looking forward to meeting everyone," Rohan said.

Kiran wasn't so sure. He'd noticed the mass of scars on his body, on his back, one arm, and his wrists. He also bore the strange round brand-like mark on the left side of his chest. The doctor had noticed them too, his mouth hardening faintly during the physical, although he hadn't said anything. Abuse hovered in his background, and Kiran had to wonder if the loss of his memory was a means of coping with reality.

ROHAN PULLED UP IN front of the sprawling house and parked beside the other cars.

Ambar leaned forward between the front seats to speak to them. "I'm excited to meet everyone but nervous too." Both emotions bubbled in her voice, and Rohan knew exactly how she felt. It was important for the Mitchells and their friends to like them and Kiran represented a possible snag in their acceptance. Not that he'd considered leaving the man in Auckland. Although they didn't know each other well, it would have felt like leaving part of him behind.

"That makes two of us," Kiran said. "What if they think I'm a danger to them?"

Rohan forced a laugh. "Both of you stop it. This is a social occasion. It's not a firing squad. Everyone will like us." He winked at Kiran. "What's not to like? We're tiger shifters. We're pretty and we're big and strong. Besides if they don't like us we'll just beat their arses."

There was a moment of startled silence when Rohan could swear he heard the grass growing.

Ambar spluttered, her mouth closing and opening. "I'm pretty, but have you looked in the mirror lately? You have black shadows under your eyes. Are you getting enough sleep?"

"Hey, I think he's pretty," Kiran said, his voice dropping to smoky and seductive.

Ambar rolled her eyes. "Don't even think about making out in the car. We want to make a good impression." With a snort of disgust, she opened the door and climbed from their vehicle.

Rohan grinned at Kiran and leaned over to brush a kiss on his lips. "Guess we'd better go and face the people."

"You'll stay with me while I talk to Saber?"

Rohan's heart turned over at the note of vulnerability in Kiran's voice. "Sure thing. You know Ambar and I researched Middlemarch before we moved here? We wouldn't have moved if we'd thought the natives were hostile."

Kiran gave a clipped nod and exited the vehicle. Rohan sighed. He knew demons haunted Kiran. Hell, if he'd lost his memory he'd worry about hidden monsters in his past. It was only natural.

Another vehicle pulled up as Rohan climbed out of the car. It was Gavin Finley and his mates.

"Hi," Gavin said. "Rohan, Kiran this is Leticia and Charlie, my mates. You must be Ambar," he added, smiling in Ambar's direction.

Leticia was slender, somewhat frail in appearance, but with a bright smile and very short blonde hair. She held a bunch of multi-colored roses, their perfume drifting to Rohan. Charlie, the cop, had equally short dark blonde hair and blue eyes. Rohan studied the pair and shook their hands. He eyed Gavin's black hair. It was cropped and a similar length as his mates' hair. Weird. Maybe it was a fashion statement. At least the natives seemed friendly.

After introductions, they all headed for the front door of the house. It opened before they could knock.

"Good! You're here," Emily said, her right hand resting on her belly. "We've been waiting for you. They're here, Saber," she called over her shoulder. "Come in."

"Sorry we're late, Emily," Leticia said, handing the roses over to Emily. "From our garden. Charlie had a callout and held us up."

"Yep, blame me," Charlie said, looking unconcerned, his eyes twinkling with good humor.

"We're not exactly on time," Rohan said. "The shop was busy. I think every single male in the district came to check out Ambar. We had an unanticipated run on microwave meals."

"I had fun." Ambar wrinkled her nose at him.

Rohan growled under his breath, the indignant feline sound making them all laugh.

"I hope you took note of names," Leticia said.

"Definitely," Emily agreed. "We'll give you the lowdown on each of them. Since it's so mild, we're sitting out in the courtyard." She made shooing motions with her free hand. "Go through so I can shut the door and put these flowers in water. They're beautiful and smell divine. Saber will organize drinks for everyone."

"Sounds good. It's been a busy day." Gavin ushered his female mate through the door, and Rohan noticed the affectionate stroke he gave her on the back. He stretched out his hand and his male mate took it without hesitation.

Ambar followed the others, but Rohan saw Kiran hesitate. He grasped Kiran's arm and drew him into the house. "Come on. We're invited," Rohan murmured. "No one is judging you."

Although Kiran followed him, Rohan sensed his tension. It was unwarranted. The Mitchells and their friends were warm and made them welcome, running through rapid introductions.

They met Saber in person—his authority as part of the Feline council obvious in his level, assessing feline-green stare. He shook each of their hands and nodded. His brothers Felix and Leo bore the same black hair and green eyes. Felix's features were almost harsh until he smiled while in Leo everything knit together into perfection. Kissed by the angels, Rohan's mother would have said.

Tomasine, Felix's mate, was petite with long black hair and a friendly smile. Isabella, an attractive blonde, was Leo's mate, and although she smiled in welcome, something about her demeanor screamed danger.

Emily arrived bearing a tray of glasses. Saber followed with a bottle of white wine and several cans of beer. He handed around drinks while Emily dispersed glasses.

"A toast," Saber said. "I want to officially welcome our new arrivals Rohan and Ambar Patel and their friend Kiran."

"You just want to marry off either Joe or Sly," Felix said. "That's why you're so happy."

Everyone laughed, and Emily said, "They'll have to hurry. Ambar said every single male in the area visited their store today."

79

"I'm sure Joe and Sly can take care of themselves," Saber said. "Although I'm glad they've settled a bit. I couldn't take any more gray hair."

Felix snorted, lines of concern digging into his harsh countenance. "At least they're males. We have a daughter. I'm getting gray hair thinking about her dating and all the randy Middlemarch males."

"You would know," Tomasine, his petite mate retorted, making everyone laugh again.

When the laughter faded, Saber raised his glass. "Welcome to Rohan, Ambar and Kiran."

"Welcome," everyone said, raising their glasses.

Emily moved to her mate's side, and he slid an arm around her waist, his hand resting on the bulge of her stomach. They smiled at each other, and Rohan started to feel like a voyeur. They had the kind of relationship he wanted. He felt a hand on his knee and drew a sharp breath. Rohan turned his head and met Kiran's intent gaze. Rohan slipped his hand over Kiran's.

Saber grinned. "We're also excited about the arrival of our child. We're open to babysitting offers." Joy blazed on Saber's face along with deep love for his mate. Rohan saw Emily smile at Saber, his return look full of the same happiness.

"To Emily and Saber," Felix said.

"To Emily and Saber," everyone repeated.

Isabella grinned. "Not long to wait now."

"Gavin said late November, early December," Emily said.

Ambar leaned over to speak to Kiran and Rohan. "This is a family celebration. Maybe we should go."

"I heard that," Emily said. "You're not leaving. We wouldn't have invited you if we didn't want you here. Besides, I want to hear about these eligible men. Were there any who looked tempting?"

"I didn't see any tempting ones," Kiran said.

"You're not meant to look," Rohan said before he thought better of the words. He needn't have feared censure. The shifters merely appeared amused, judging by their grins.

"There's no harm in looking," Emily said. "It's when the touching starts you need to worry."

"Emily!" Tomasine said.

Rohan didn't listen to the rest of the laughter and good-natured insults. He was too busy concentrating on Kiran. "You looked at other men."

"Yes. I wondered if my...injuries and gratitude were blinding me."

Pain seared through Rohan, slicing straight through the warmth and companionship he'd felt earlier. He stood abruptly and set his drink aside.

"No wait," Kiran said. "You didn't give me time to finish." He stood and grabbed Rohan's hand. "Emily," he murmured, stepping away from his fear for the first time since their arrival at the Mitchells. "Is it all right if we explore your garden?"

"Of course. Feel free," she said. "Saber, it's time to put on the steaks. Can I have some volunteers to help bring out the salads and plates? Luckily, the weather is cooperating. It's been a very mild winter."

Thanks to Emily everyone burst into action, taking the focus off them.

Kiran's hand tightened on his and tugged him to the far end of the garden. They left the cobblestone area, stepping onto springy grass. Over to their right, several vegetable beds of early lettuce, beetroot, and broccoli obviously provided the family with plenty of fresh food.

"I didn't mean to hurt you," Kiran said. "I wanted to make sure the things I've been feeling around you weren't an anomaly."

"What things?"

"You know what things," Kiran said.

"Tell me again so we're both clear." Rohan didn't attempt to hide the snap in his voice.

"When I'm around you I feel as if I'm going to jump from my skin. I want to touch you, kiss you. Fuck you. I think about that a lot. I needed to be sure in my own mind."

Rohan's shoulders slumped with relief. "So you're not going to leave me? You're not going to look at other men? Or women?"

Kiran's smiled. "I'll stay as long as you want me to." The smile faltered. "You might not want me once my memory returns." His unease returned, his throat working in a swallow. "If my memory returns."

The forlorn note in his voice pulled Rohan out of the lingering jealousy. "It doesn't matter to me if you remember your past or not. We can make new memories together."

"What did I do to deserve you?"

"It's fate. Kismet," Rohan said. "I'm not about to screw with that."

"CAN I SLEEP WITH you tonight?" Kiran asked.

Rohan grasped his hand, drawn by the diffidence in Kiran's face and voice. "Yeah." He turned to his sister. "Ambar, you have a problem with Kiran and me sharing a room?"

"No problem." She paused outside her bedroom door, her mouth curling up in an impish grin. "Try to keep the noise down, huh?" She slipped inside her bedroom and closed the door. They both heard her chuckle, and the sound warmed Rohan as much as Kiran's request.

"I'm glad your bedroom is at the other end of the passage," Kiran said.

"Yeah, we could always buy her some earplugs." Lust swept his body as his gaze strummed over Kiran. "I don't want to talk about Ambar." His words emerged clipped. Abrupt.

"What do you want to talk about?"

"What I want doesn't involve talking. Your mouth will be too busy for talking."

Kiran nodded, the color in his cheeks deepening a fraction. "Works for me."

Unable to resist, Rohan backed him against the wall and started kissing him. Rohan loved the softness of Kiran's mouth, the way he sometimes took boldly while at others he let Rohan take and seemed to enjoy the passive role. Rohan ran his tongue across Kiran's bottom lip, knowing the rough texture of his tongue would start Kiran's nerves hopping.

Kiran groaned, his hands rising to spear his fingers through Rohan's hair. He gripped him tight, fingers tugging to the point of pain. Rohan growled and nipped his lip. The coppery taste of blood brought him back to his senses, and he jerked away from Kiran, worry pounding him. Kiran didn't move. His eyes seemed unfocused, his color pale. If Rohan didn't know better, he'd call it shock.

"Damn, I'm sorry. You okay? Let me see." Rohan moved cautiously, not wanting to frighten Kiran but needing to reassure himself that he hadn't bitten too hard. He didn't think he had. The bleeding wasn't too bad.

"Will you two get a room?" Ambar shouted. "I can hear you. And you'd better be talking about hands or something respectable because I'm coming out to grab my book from the kitchen."

Ambar's shout pulled Kiran back to the present. A shudder went through him and he blinked.

"You okay?" Rohan asked, putting his hands on Kiran's shoulders. He squeezed carefully, taking care to temper his strength.

"What happened?"

"I got carried away and bit your lip. When you tasted the blood, you zoned out. Worried me, man."

Ambar's bedroom door opened and she cautiously poked her head out. "Good. You're decent." She scuttled out, wearing a long pale blue robe, and returned a couple of minutes later bearing a romance with a lurid cover. "They're about to do the deed," she announced, waving the book. "I have to know what happens next."

"As long as you don't get any ideas," Rohan muttered.

"Oh I have ideas," Ambar purred. "Putting them into practice might take a bit longer." The door shut behind her with a loud click.

"Your sister is going to lead some man on a real dance," Kiran said.

Relief hit Rohan, and he tugged Kiran down the passage toward his bedroom. "It will be fun watching from the sidelines, but I almost feel as if I should warn prospective males. She's come out of her shell since my parents died. They were very strict, particularly with Ambar."

Once inside his bedroom, Rohan shut the door and turned on the light. He stalked past the pile of boxes and the suitcase he hadn't had a chance to unpack and spun around to face Kiran. "You didn't answer my question. Did I hurt you?"

"No." Kiran averted his gaze.

Rohan bit back the retort tickling his lips and dragged in a deep breath instead. "Have you remembered something?"

"Yeah. I don't like blood."

Okay. Fair enough. Damn, his cock ached something fierce. Rohan resisted the urge to yank on his jeans. "Do you still want to sleep with me?"

"Yes."

But he'd killed the mood. Kiran wasn't in the mood for sex now.

Cursing under his breath, Rohan removed his shirt and the rest of his clothes and footwear. After a quick trip to the adjoining bathroom to brush his teeth, he pulled back the covers and switched on the bedside lamp.

Kiran watched Rohan prowl across the room, noting the tension in his cock. His stomach turned a slow somersault while he studied Rohan. Things had been going fine, he'd enjoyed Rohan touching and kissing him. Until the blood. The taste of it had brought terror, the color of red shrouding his sight and dragging him into a silent abyss. Ambar had wrenched him back with her loud shouts through the door, and now Rohan was treating him like a leper.

Rohan stretched out on the bed and glanced at him. "You want me to leave the light on for you?"

"It's fine. I can see without." Kiran walked through to their shared bathroom and cleaned his teeth. What the hell had happened to him? He didn't understand. He'd dreamed about blood and hadn't flipped out the way he had with Rohan. With his tongue, he explored the cut on the inside of his bottom lip. Tender. A little sore but it wasn't bleeding.

Kiran headed back to Rohan's bedroom and hesitated at the doorway, wondering if he should return to his own room. Rohan was pissed at him, and he couldn't blame him. Erratic behavior. Hell, he had that down.

"Are you coming to bed, or are you going to stare at me all night?" The grumpy voice cut through the dark and made him jump.

"I'm deciding," Kiran said in a firm voice.

"Don't think too hard. You'll keep me awake."

"Why are you angry with me?" Kiran thought he knew and wanted confirmation.

"I'm not angry with you."

"But you are angry."

"I'm furious with myself for pushing too hard. It can't be easy for you, not knowing who you are, and all I can think of is fucking you. What you need now is a friend not a lover."

Kiran swallowed. "Can't I have both?"

Rohan turned over to face him, his eyes glowing in the dark. He didn't try to hide his feline nature, and that reassured Kiran. He stripped rapidly and climbed into the bed, sliding over until their naked bodies touched.

Rohan's arms wrapped around him, and Kiran sighed, the rough breath sounding like a purr of contentment.

"We'll slow down, like we decided at the start, get to know one another."

That wasn't what Kiran wanted, and although he suspected in the past he would have accepted the decision made by another, he didn't want to today. Or maybe it was his dream that had affected him. In the dream, he'd been a slave. He hadn't liked the feeling.

"No," he said, the word loud in the silent room. "I don't want slow. I want to go with the moment, do what feels right."

"And if I do something that scares you?"

Kiran pressed a kiss to Rohan's chest, drawing the other man's scent deep into his lungs. "I'll get over it."

"But if I scar you for life?"

"Gavin said my memory might come back, but what if it doesn't? I can't creep through life frightened of something in my past. Something I might never remember."

"I hear you," Rohan said, his warm breath puffing over Kiran's neck.

Kiran had difficulty suppressing his reaction, and his body started to react to the touch, blood filling his cock. He rocked his hips, letting out a groan when his shaft slid across Rohan's belly. It felt so good he did it again, this time leaving a wet trail.

"Yes." Kiran's eyes closed while he soaked up the pleasure. He felt Rohan kiss him on the chin, a soft open-mouthed caress designed to soothe. Instead it ramped up the urgency between them. Their bodies strained against each other, hands clenched and hips arched, aligned so their cocks brushed and slid together, the friction bringing heated groans.

"Are you sure you want this?" Rohan asked.

"Yes." Kiran tensed, worried Rohan would back away again. It was the last thing he wanted. He kissed him, only relaxing when Rohan clutched his shoulders and started to participate without hesitation. Relief filled Kiran, and he relaxed, settling in to enjoy the experience. When Rohan reached down to grasp his cock, he paused. "Both," he said. "Get both of us off at the same time."

Rohan didn't hesitate, rubbing their dicks together, using tight, hard strokes.

Pleasure soared through Kiran, making him feel as if he were flying. The pressure in his balls increased, the musky scent and harsh breathing drawing them together in a sensual bubble. Rohan's hand stroked across the crown and the tension inside Kiran snapped. His hips canted upward, and he let out a low moan as the orgasmic buzz hurled him into ecstasy.

"Damn, you look hot when you do that," Rohan growled.

The continual pump of Rohan's hand across the head of Kiran's cock was almost too much for him, but he didn't protest. Instead, he dipped his head and kissed across Rohan's chest, dragging his tongue over a nipple.

A hungry noise escaped Rohan, and Kiran immediately repeated the move, scraping his teeth across the nub this time. Rohan tensed and seconds later hot spurts of semen splashed against Kiran's stomach. Kiran pressed against Rohan's chest, ignoring the uncomfortable stickiness. He was right where he wanted to be.

MUMBAI, INDIA

David Marsters exited the limousine with his briefcase in hand and a spring in his step. Away from home for a month in London on business, he was looking forward to a rest. And sex, he thought, his body tightening with anticipation. He'd tried not to think about his slave, but the man had burrowed into his heart. This slave wasn't like the others. He didn't show fear and he followed every order. A slow smile bloomed. The sex, the pleasure…

The time away from India had been necessary, and knowing the authorities wouldn't approve of his proclivities, he'd had to leave his slaves at home. Of course he'd arranged prostitutes to fill his needs, but it wasn't the same as having his favorite slave at his beck and call for his personal pleasure.

By the time he reached the side door into the house, a servant waited to take his briefcase and to see to his comfort. The scents of spices and flowers, the slower cadence of life in Mumbai eased the last of his tension.

"Have a bath drawn and send my slave to tend me."

"Yes, sir."

David took the stairs to the master bedroom two at a time. Inside, he stripped off his suit jacket and tossed it on the end of the bed. Discarding the rest of his clothes and footwear, he strode to the window and looked out at the garden. His laugh filled the room when he realized he was nervous. Because of a slave!

A timid knock on the door made him turn. His smile died, replaced by a scowl.

"Where is my slave?"

The woman cowered at his tone. "He…he is gone."

A red haze speared David's mind. With two giant steps, he was on the woman, his hands around her neck. He squeezed and tossed her aside when she started to gasp and struggle.

Naked, he took a few steps before returning to his room to grab a robe. There was an explanation for this. He should have asked about the slaves when he rang. He'd wanted to but had refrained, not liking to show weakness to his younger brothers. They nipped at his heels like a pack of rabid wolves, each of them ready to seize control and step into his shoes. The last thing he wanted them to know was how much he cared for the slave, how he craved the man's touch, hungered for it.

"Ah, David. You are home." His youngest brother passed him in the passage, the best of all his four siblings.

"Yes. I must see to my staff."

His brother frowned. "There was some trouble while you were away." He glanced over his shoulder and drew David into a guest chamber.

When David went to speak, his brother stopped him. Mystified, David followed him into the bathroom and watched him turn both the shower and the tap on before whispering to him.

"I don't have much time. The others are going to tell you several of the slaves died when a virus passed through the slave quarters. It's not true. Something happened. I don't know what, but the slave—the one you favor most—disappeared one night. I didn't like to ask questions. They slaughtered other slaves and kept the rest locked up, saying the virus was contagious."

David kept a tight lid on his anger. This time his brothers had gone too far. For years he'd ignored their criminal dealings. Besides, it wasn't as if he could cast stones. Following the laws of the land didn't make for comfortable living, and he liked the niceties of life.

"Why are you telling me? And don't you think you're paranoid? This is our home. It's swept regularly for listening devices."

"Can't be too careful." A flicker of discomfort crossed his youngest brother's face and he glanced away. "I don't like living this way. It's not right and I intend to change. I'm leaving today. I wanted to say goodbye."

"You're going on holiday?" David stared hard at his brother, willing direct eye contact again. "When will you be back?"

"I'm not coming back. I'm moving into an apartment."

"That's great." The set of his brother's face told David he meant it. "But what's the big secret? Why are you intending to sneak away?"

"The others are out of control. They have no concept of right or wrong, and by staying here I'm showing approval of their actions. I'm not willing to lie any longer." His younger brother shut off the water, signaling their conversation had ended. He left the guest room and walked away without looking back. David watched until he disappeared, uneasy with his words and behavior. Despite having the same father, he didn't know his younger brother well because of the fifteen years between them.

The brothers between them were closer in years, close period since they spent all their time together.

Fury, lying idle while he'd spoken to his brother, sprang to life. David stormed down the passage to find his other brothers.

He found them in the courtyard, lolling on loungers by the pool. A servant delivered food and drinks as he arrived.

David didn't even wait for the servant to depart. "Where is my slave?" he demanded in an icy voice.

"I don't know what you're talking about," Suman said.

Isa and Jay laughed, and David caught the sly looks between them.

"What?" he snarled.

"Why do you care? He's a slave. There are others."

David took a slow breath and let it ease out, knowing he had to hold it together. He couldn't afford to show weakness. "He is trained. I have limited time to train replacements."

Suman snickered and muttered something to the brother next to him.

"I'm in charge here," David snarled, not bothering to temper his fury this time. "The slaves are my responsibility."

"He's dead. A virus. Things seem to be under control now. We haven't had any more deaths since we disposed of the bodies."

"What were the symptoms of this virus?"

Isa sniggered. "Spots on the chest."

David narrowed his eyes, and his brother became silent. "Spots of blood, perchance? Yeah, not laughing now are you? Don't touch the slaves again without my permission."

"How are you going to stop us?"

"Try me and find out." David's voice was hard and mean and their faces paled. He turned and stalked away, heading to the slave quarters. He'd question them, the overseer and take things from there. If his slave was really dead there would be hell to pay.

"What happened?" he demanded of the overseer when he found him in his quarters.

"Your brothers requested several slaves for private use. They told me to send all twelve, so I did. Only eight returned. The male slave you favor was one of those missing."

An ache started in David's chest. "Could he have escaped?"

"No, the alarms were set. The security guards would have noticed."

David nodded. "Let me talk to them."

Half an hour later, David was none the wiser. He made his way to the master bedroom and cast aside his robe. Slipping into the tepid water of the prepared bath, he sank back and closed his eyes. Fatigue made his mind sluggish. Despite the luxury of the first-class seat, he hadn't managed much sleep on the flight from Heathrow to India. Damn, he missed his slave. The man had looks and an innate sexiness despite his poor upbringing. He was intelligent and, thanks to David, well-educated. David's cock lengthened at the thought of tunneling into the slave's ass, the tight heat and the pulsating grip on his shaft.

"The tracker. Hell." He sat up abruptly, the fog of fatigue dropping away. He washed rapidly and stood, the water cascading off his body. After grabbing a towel and roughly drying his body, David opened his briefcase and set up his laptop. When he attained new slaves, he arranged a physical and had the doctor implant a tracker in the slave's neck. He'd never needed to follow any of the trackers before.

David tapped several computer keys and anxiously watched the screen. Nothing. His shoulders slumped until a thought occurred. If his slave was dead, the tracker would show in the place where the family usually disposed of bodies. It didn't show on the screen at all, which meant the slave wasn't in range. David doubted the slave had found and removed the tracker because it was so minute. Which meant it was possible his slave was alive. An outside chance, yes, but he wouldn't give up yet.

Of course he could train other slaves, but he'd become attached to this one.

His bottom lip curled in self-mockery. Yeah, he was rather afraid his feelings were stronger and edging close to love. A weakness for others to exploit. Now that could make things interesting...

KIRAN SLIPPED INTO SLEEP and the nightmare started straightaway. Blood. It poured from his bottom lip.

The master held his head still, his dark eyes sparkling with lust. "Beautiful," he murmured, his white teeth covered with Kiran's blood. His cock speared into Kiran's hip, palpable excitement clutching the man's body.

He loved pushing boundaries and bringing the edge of violence to sex.

Kiran shivered inside with fear and fought to keep his breathing even. He'd ended up in the master's clutches, plucked from the streets after his mother's death. The master had taken him in, educating and training him as a sex slave.

The master nuzzled his neck, using the sharp edge of his teeth.

Kiran concentrated on the one spot of sunshine in his life, a fellow slave Rajah, who shared a bed with him. Friend.

The master bit down on his shoulder like a vampire, dragging Kiran from his happy spot into reality. He groaned, felt the trickle of blood down his shoulder. As if his groan was a sign, the master pulled on a condom, roughly spread his legs, and guided his cock to Kiran's hole. He pushed steadily while Kiran struggled to relax and take him. At least the master had used lube on his cock and repeated penetration over the last year had made it easier for Kiran. He kept his eyes fixed on the master's face—an attractive face if one ignored the flashes of cruelty and the implacable will beneath the urbanity.

The master liked obedience, and that's what Kiran gave him.

The master stroked into his body, his eyes squeezed shut, his face full of open pleasure. He used slow, even thrusts, angling slightly to hit Kiran's gland. The master liked to bring Kiran pleasure and gave as well as took. Kiran didn't understand it, hated the way his body reacted, the way his cock enlarged and his scrotum tightened.

The master liked his reaction. It made the man's cock swell, his breath come faster.

"Come for me, Kiran. Come for me." The master quivered and grasped Kiran's cock. He withdrew and slammed home, the extra stimulation of cock pushing him into climax. Trembles and shakes took him, the hard spurts of semen bringing a shout of delight from the master. He increased the speed of his pumps and stilled, a loud moan coming from deep in his chest. Heedless of the sticky mess of Kiran's chest, he collapsed against his body, his breath labored and hoarse.

"No one makes me come like you," the master said. "Thank you."

The master was a big man, Kiran's equal in size, his body heavy. Kiran fought to breathe but didn't move or protest. He knew better. The master had killed one of the slaves a few months ago for voicing a protest.

Thankfully the master moved, pulling from his body. "Prepare a bath for me," he said, removing the condom and handing it to Kiran. "Wash yourself and come back when you're clean." The master moved to a dry spot, sprawling out with easy grace.

Kiran nodded respectfully and hastened to complete the master's orders. In the luxurious bathroom, he dreamed of escape, of freedom. He dreamed of a day when he could do whatever he wanted when he wanted. The master called.

Kiran padded into the bedroom and halted by the bed. "Yes, master."

"Clean me then suck me off."

Obediently, Kiran went for a cloth and cleansed his cock then knelt by the side of the bed and grasped his master's erection. One day he would walk in freedom. One day...

Chapter Five

"When we were at the Mitchells last night I asked about somewhere to run," Ambar said. "Saber said we could run on their property and told me exactly how to get to a safe place. All we need to do is ring first to let them know we intend to run. Would you both like to go tonight after dinner? It's been so long," she added.

Rohan grinned at Kiran, raising his brows in a silent question.

Kiran couldn't remember running in feline form, not even the faint sense of having done it before. "I'm not even sure I can shift." What if he couldn't change to his feline and Rohan rejected him? The negative thought popped into his head before he could stop it. He couldn't seem to halt the self-destructive thoughts, the fear of losing Rohan. Every time he saw Rohan, the feline drew him. He wanted to touch and rub against Rohan until they both purred.

"You shifted after escaping from the zoo, or at least we think you did. You won't have any problems." Rohan sounded confident, and Kiran wished he shared the sentiment. He sidled closer to Rohan, craving physical reassurance, relief easing out in a sigh when Rohan swung an arm around his shoulders in a loose embrace.

"This is an ideal opportunity to find out," Ambar said with an encouraging smile. "And if there are problems we'll be able to let Gavin know."

"Okay," Kiran said, forcing a calm nod in return. Inside he felt anything but composed with nerves battering his confidence. The disappearance of his memory left him uncertain about day-to-day things. The only time he felt safe was when he was with Rohan.

"Great, that's decided." Ambar checked her watch and strode across the sparkling terracotta tiles to open the front door of the store. "I'll square it with Saber. Oh for goodness sake," she muttered.

"What's wrong?"

"There are three males out there all glaring at each other. It looks as if punches will fly any second. What is wrong with the men around here?" She sniffed, her mouth pursing in disdain. "Feline. I should have guessed. That's it. I refuse to date a feline male. They're just...stupid. What I need is a human."

"Ambar!" Rohan said.

A bark of laughter forced its way up Kiran's throat. He couldn't help it. He loved the interactions between brother and sister. A wave of anxiety flickered through him, replacing his good humor. If he and Rohan chose to pursue a relationship, Ambar would need to accept him without reservation. His past might make a difference.

"Don't encourage her," Rohan said. "Ambar doesn't have any idea how difficult life would be dating a human."

"It couldn't be any more difficult than dating a feline," Ambar said, turning the lock and switching the sign to open. "Don't think I haven't noticed the way you two circle each other, so don't try to give me advice."

The bell tinkled on the door and the three males pushed their way inside in a mini stampede.

"Morning, gentlemen," Rohan said. "Ambar, did you want to make that phone call now?"

"Good idea," she said, not looking at any of the three. "Call me if you need me."

"I wanted to ask you something," one of the feline men called.

"I'm sorry," Ambar said sweetly. "I promised my boyfriend I'd call him this morning. He gets a bit edgy if he doesn't hear from me."

"You're mated?"

Kiran watched the entire scene with amazement. He knew Ambar wasn't mated, but instead of answering or lying any more than she had already, she merely sniffed and walked away. If she'd been in tiger form, her tail would have twitched.

"My sister is independent," Rohan said. "She makes her own choices and doesn't appreciate males crowding her." His voice held a thread of warning, and Kiran stepped up beside him to present a united front. Together they stared at the males until they gave way. Two left and the third grabbed a shopping basket and stomped down the toiletry aisle.

Rohan grabbed his arm and winked at him. "I can't wait to run with you tonight. It will be fine. You'll see. Don't worry about your dreams either. They might be pure fiction. Besides, you said you didn't dream last night. That's good, right?"

"Yes." A pang of guilt ran through Kiran. He should have told Rohan the truth but didn't like to worry him. The one consistent thread in his dreams was the master and the fact Kiran was his sexual slave. "I'll start restocking the shelves," he said, turning away to hide his unease.

"You don't have to," Rohan said.

Kiran turned back. "I know I don't. I like to keep busy, and you and Ambar have been so good to me. If I can do something to help in return, I will. I'm doing this because I want to."

"We both like having you around," Rohan said, sincerity ringing in his voice.

"Thanks."

A customer walked over to the checkout area, claiming Rohan's attention, and Kiran scanned the nearby shelves, checking to see what needed restocking. Kiran worked steadily throughout the morning until Ambar tapped him on the shoulder.

"I have a craving for a latte. Do you want to walk to Storm in a Teacup with me?"

Kiran glanced at Rohan, who was serving a customer. "What about Rohan?"

Ambar smirked in her brother's direction. "I'm going to steal his man for half an hour. Let him be curious." She grabbed her purse, slipped the strap over one shoulder, and linked arms with Kiran. "Rohan, Kiran, and I are going for a coffee. Do you want us to bring one back for you?"

"Do you have to drag Kiran off with you?"

Ambar giggled. "I need an escort in case some of Middlemarch's pesky males try to grab me. Consider Kiran protection."

"Huh, you're quite capable of taking care of yourself," Rohan said.

"Bye!" Ambar dragged Kiran from the store, laughing. "Come on."

"Why do you and Rohan trust me? I could be anyone." The words burst from him and Ambar glanced at him in surprise.

"You make Rohan happy. What more do I need to know? Stop worrying so much, Kiran. Just accept you're with friends who want you and live for the moment. Life's too short to stress."

"Thanks." Her words humbled Kiran and raised guilt again.

Up ahead he saw Gavin and Charlie walk into the café. Maybe he should talk to Gavin about the dreams. Still mulling the idea over, he allowed Ambar to steer him across the road and into the café.

Three tourists left the café as they entered, taking their bikes and pedaling toward the start of the cycle track. Kiran and Ambar stepped inside, the scent of coffee and fresh bread drifting through the air to welcome them.

Several of the indoor tables were full, and Kiran could see three small boys running around outside, in hot pursuit of each other while their parents looked on and drank coffee at the outdoor tables.

"Hey," Charlie said, lifting his hand in a wave. "Gavin and I came for a quick coffee before Gavin goes on rounds. Do you want to join us?"

"Sure thing," Ambar said. "Kiran, a latte okay with you?"

He nodded, although he had no idea if he liked latte or not.

"How are you doing?" Gavin asked.

A frown slipped onto Kiran's face. He glanced at Charlie.

"I'll go and help Ambar with the coffee," Charlie said. "I promised Leticia a chocolate brownie anyway."

Kiran waited until Charlie left. "I wondered if I could come and talk to you."

"I have to go out on calls for the rest of the day. Animals," Gavin said.

"It doesn't matter. It can wait."

Gavin leaned back in his chair. "Why don't you come with me? We can talk between my jobs, and I'll give you a tour at the same time."

"Are you sure that's okay? What about your mates?"

"What about his mates?" Charlie asked, pulling out his chair and joining them again.

"I don't want to step on any toes," Kiran said.

"Hold that thought right there," Gavin said. "Charlie and Leticia won't mind you doing rounds with me."

"Unless you intend to go crazy and attack him," Charlie said. "He's a pain in the butt at times, but we love him."

"Thanks," Gavin said, his tone dry. "Kiran is going to be my assistant this afternoon."

Charlie's brows shot up toward his hairline. "Does he know what he's letting himself in for? The last time I helped Gavin he was sticking his hands up the rear ends of cows."

"I'm doing inoculations mostly," Gavin said, grinning at the horror etched into Charlie's face.

"I think it's a good idea. Rohan won't mind," Ambar said, sliding into the fourth seat at the table. "You can give us all the local gossip tonight."

A bark of laughter escaped Charlie. "Gavin doesn't gossip. Leticia and I are always the last to hear everything."

Charlie's words reassured Kiran and made him decide to trust Gavin. He needed to talk to someone, and since Gavin had medical expertise, it made sense for Kiran to talk to him. He hated to worry either Rohan or Ambar when they'd been so good to him and risked exposure to rescue him from the hospital.

Kiran stressed increasingly about his past because the dreams had to mean something. He loathed what he saw, the man he was, and the life he'd lived. After his talk with Gavin, he'd decide whether to stay or walk away. The last thing he wanted was to bring danger into Rohan and Ambar's lives, yet his gut screamed he was doing exactly that by staying with them.

To his surprise, Rohan encouraged him to go out with Gavin, showing not the slightest amount of jealousy.

"Make sure you keep an eye out for eligible males for Ambar," he murmured in a low voice.

"I heard that," Ambar shouted from the far end of the store. "Don't even think of reporting back to my brother. You report directly to me if you see any possible candidates. You hear?"

"I should think they can hear in Auckland," Rohan said.

"While you're listening, I'd like to add I'm perfectly capable of choosing a mate. I'm not flighty or a stupid giggly high school girl. I know what I want in a mate, and I don't need you to replace our parents as morality police. Did you hear that?" Ambar sauntered down the aisle to join them at the counter.

"Heard and digested." Rohan winked at Kiran. "But that won't stop me from offering my ten cents of opinion every time a male comes within spitting distance."

"Which gives me equal rights," Ambar said sweetly. "Have a good time. I'm looking forward to our run. Maybe Gavin and his mates will come with us. It would be good to have a female along."

Kiran glanced at Rohan. "Do you want me to ask?"

"Yeah, although isn't Charlie a human?" Rohan asked.

Ambar tossed her French braid over her shoulder. "You still have to issue the invitation to all of them."

"I think it would be fun, and it might be good to have Gavin there in case you have problems."

Kiran scowled. "I'm not an invalid."

Ambar touched his forearm. "Of course you're not, but Rohan and I worry. Humor us, please."

The words and Rohan's intent gaze warmed him inside, and a cautious smile hovered, pushing against his cheek muscles. Somehow he didn't think people had cared for him in the past. "Okay. I'll see you later. I'm meeting Gavin at his surgery. We'll be back around six unless there's an emergency somewhere."

Ambar waved and Rohan closed the distance between them, planting a hard kiss on his lips. Kiran's hands curled around his shoulders, drawing him closer and softening against Rohan. Immediately Rohan gentled his kiss, coaxing instead of demanding. The warmth inside Kiran grew. He really liked this man. Every time they touched, it was magic, making Kiran want to return the sentiment a hundredfold. He could imagine a future with Rohan and that scared and thrilled him.

Rohan pulled back, brushing his fingertips over the bristly stubble on Kiran's cheek. He winked. "Hold that thought."

Nodding, Kiran left the store with a smile on his face. It lasted for the entire five-minute walk to the surgery. He pushed open the door to the surgery and stepped inside.

"Good timing," Gavin said. "Can you give me a hand to carry out this stuff?"

"Sure." Kiran picked up the two boxes Gavin indicated and followed him outside to a muddy SUV. They loaded the vaccine in the back before climbing inside.

"Before I forget, Saber said we could go for a run on their property. It's been a while for Rohan and Ambar, and they're keen to go tonight. They wondered if you and your mates would like to come with us."

"Great idea," Gavin said. "I can't speak for Leticia and Charlie but I'm in."

"I haven't tried to shift since Rohan and Ambar found me in the hospital. Do you think it will be all right? I can't remember how to shift," he confessed.

"You're probably overthinking the process," Gavin said. "You're in good health, apart from being underweight for your height. Don't worry, the shifting will come back to you." He turned onto a gravel road, the bumps becoming increasingly worse as they progressed up a hill. The tussock land gave way to pines, the scent of dust to tangy sap and pine.

"I've been having lots of dreams. They're about the same person and I'm in them." His voice cracked and he had to swallow before attempting to get out the rest. "In my dreams, I'm a sexual slave." Shame crawled through him at the confession, and he wasn't sure where to look, how Gavin would react.

"It might explain some of the old scars on your back and the rest of your body," Gavin said.

Kiran's face grew hot with humiliation. He didn't want to mention the embarrassing details from his dreams. The way he'd acted so submissively and done nothing to help the other slaves. "What if these dreams are my reality?"

"That scares you?"

"Hell, yeah," Kiran growled, finally risking a glance at Gavin. To his surprise, instead of disgust, he saw understanding and sympathy. It encouraged him to continue. "Rohan and Ambar are great. They risked themselves to help me. I can't help thinking my past is going to bring trouble for them."

"You're giving them something back," Gavin said.

Kiran snorted. "I help them in the store. That's nothing compared to what they've given me."

"Rohan cares for you. The attraction between you is palpable."

"But I don't know my sexual history. I don't know anything about my past."

"We all have pasts. They're what shape us and make us into productive adults. Medically you're healthy. Safe. You don't need to worry about spreading anything to Rohan." Gavin turned into a driveway that was nothing more than a dirt track. If anything, the bumps were worse. They clattered over a cattle stop, driving past a wooden bungalow-style house and came to a stop by a set of yards.

"First stop," Gavin said.

"What do you want me to do? I don't think I know anything about animals."

"Bullshit," Gavin said. "You're a tiger. You have instincts."

"Don't the animals sense your feline?" Kiran asked, watching the cattle milling around inside the yard with interest. He had no recollection of the countryside, which meant he must live in a city or town. Maybe.

"Some of the animals do. I've been at Middlemarch for a while now. The ones I visit on a regular basis are used to me. There are lots of feline farmers around here so the animals don't know anything else."

A harried woman appeared from the direction of the farmhouse. She carried a bawling toddler on her hip. Another child clung to her leg, peeking around the baggy sweatpants and sucking her thumb at the same time. "Frank has been held up in Mosgiel and won't be able to get back to help. He asked if you could let the cattle out and come back next week."

Gavin glanced at Kiran. "I have an assistant with me today. We can cope and that will save Frank from having to worry about mustering again next week."

"Really?" A smile of relief and quiet gratitude lit the woman's tired face. "That would be wonderful. I've made scones. Stop by for a cup of tea when you're done. Just let the cattle out into the paddock once you're finished. There's plenty of water and enough feed until Frank gets home."

"Will do," Gavin said.

Kiran waited until the woman left. "Assistant?"

"Yep. We'll put a few head in the race at a time, inoculate them and repeat the process until we're done. No sweat."

"Whatever you say." The other feline's matter-of-fact assumption that he'd help and do a good job boosted his confidence. How hard could it be?

Harder than Kiran thought. The cattle were plain skittish, resisting entry to the race. Frustrated by their obstinate natures, on the fourth attempt Kiran started talking to them in his mind. *It's only a race. All you need to do is go through, and we'll let you out the other end.*

To Kiran's shock, thoughts flashed in his head, thoughts he hadn't put there.

Pain. Sore.

A cow mooed, a low, complaining sound. The others joined in with the first.

Hurt.

A quick injection. It will stop you from getting sick, he replied in his thoughts.

"That's weird," Gavin said. "I've never seen them act like this before."

Kiran cast them a quick glance and checked on Gavin. "Maybe it's me." *Do you want to get sick? Have your calves get sick? You need the shots.*

One cow walked over to him and rubbed her head against his chest. He stood motionless, smelling the dirt beneath their feet, the pines, and the animal scent of the cattle. He stroked his hand over her shoulder, she made a snuffling sound and turned toward the race, walking calmly inside and waiting at the gate at the other end.

Each of the cattle walked up to Kiran and rubbed against him before following the lead cow. When the race was full, the rest waited in line.

"You gonna start soon?" Kiran asked.

"I don't believe it." Gavin shook his head and blinked once then again. He frowned at the line of cattle. "That was the weirdest thing I've ever seen. You'd better shut the gate at this end of the race."

Do I need to shut the gate?

The lead cow mooed. Kiran turned back to Gavin. "I don't think you'll need to do that."

"Whatever you say," Gavin said, sounding bemused. He grabbed the vaccines and started work. The cattle stood quietly for him. When he got to the end of the line in the race, he paused. "I'll let them out of the race."

"Why don't you try injecting them here? They're all standing quiet," Kiran said.

Ten minutes later, they'd finished, and Kiran opened the gates for the cattle to exit the yards.

Gavin watched them go, many of them rubbing against Kiran before they left.

"Okay," Gavin said when the last animal left the yards. "How did you do that?"

"I started muttering to them in my thoughts and suddenly I could hear what they were thinking."

Gavin spluttered a laugh. "You can talk to the animals?"

Kiran lifted his shoulders in a shrug. "Crazy, huh? I didn't know I could do that."

"What did they say to you?"

"It was more like single words rather than complete thoughts."

"Man, that's crazy. I wish I could do that. It would make my job a lot easier." Gavin picked up an empty box, now full of discarded vials. "It's getting to the stage when I could do with an assistant. Not many felines train as vets, and I've been reluctant to hire a human because of some of the sensitive stuff in my lab at the surgery. You're a hell of a find. What do you say to working with me?"

"But you don't know anything about my past. I haven't told you about my dreams yet. They're not pretty."

"I know enough to see you're great with animals. That's all I need to know because animals are great judges of character. If you want a job with me, you have it. Part-time if you want. I can't afford to pay much."

Gavin's job offer left him speechless. Kiran stared at the feline for an instant then nodded. "I need to talk to Rohan and Ambar first."

Gavin slapped him heartily on the back, his grin holding warmth. "There's no hurry. Let's go and have our cup of tea."

By the end of the day, Kiran had worked out he could communicate with most four-legged animals. The flock of geese at the last farm had hissed at him and attacked. Gavin had about killed himself laughing as they chased Kiran across the paddock.

"See you around eight," Kiran said when Gavin dropped him off outside the store.

With a wave, Gavin drove off, and Kiran walked into the store.

Ambar wrinkled her nose when she saw him. "Eew, did you bring half the farm back with you? You stink."

Rohan smirked, remaining at a safe distance. "She's right about the stinky part. Maybe you should go back to the house and grab a shower. Ambar, I'm gonna take a break."

"It's almost closing time anyway," she said, "but if a group of single men comes in all bets are off. I'll ring for help."

"Deal," Kiran said, holding the door to the store open for Rohan. "We'll protect you."

"You're in a good mood," Rohan said. "Did you have a good time?"

"Yeah." Kiran released the door and fell into step with Rohan as they headed for the house. "Gavin offered me a job as his assistant. He said I'm a natural."

"That's great," Rohan said, beaming. "You're gonna take the job, right?"

Kiran halted to wait for a car before crossing the road, his shoulder bumping against Rohan's in comfortable companionship. "I said I'd talk to you and Ambar first. You've been so good to me. I wanted to check to see if it's okay to keep staying with you here in Middlemarch. I mean I could always find my own place if you didn't want me around."

"Why wouldn't we want you around?" Anger blazed on Rohan's face, even more noticeable because he usually bore a smile. He jerked away from Kiran and glared at him. "Fuck, Kiran," he snarled. "How can you ask that? I want you. I can't be much plainer than that. I want to mate with you formally. I don't give a flying fuck about your past. All I want is today and tomorrow. A future. I've been trying to go slow, holding back because I didn't think it was fair to push you. Surely you must have realized the way I feel about you?"

Only then Kiran realized the tension he held in his body. Rohan's words eased it away, leaving him full of anticipation. Every time Rohan touched him he went up in flames. Every time he looked at Rohan, he wanted to move closer, to touch and taste. Kiran's breath eased out in a hiss. Oh yeah. Tasting was on the menu.

"Well, fuck you," Rohan snapped, his face contorted in fury and underlying pain. He opened the door to the house and stomped inside.

Kiran grabbed his shoulder and whirled Rohan around to face him, halting his departure. "I'd like to." He didn't smile or cajole, just stared at Rohan, memorizing the angles and curves of his face. When Rohan continued to glare, Kiran sighed. "I'm sorry. I'm not handling this well. My past worries me. I know my English is good, I'm reasonably educated, but every gut instinct tells me my background isn't pretty. What happens if my memory returns and I change? What then?"

A derisive snort emerged from Rohan, but at least the rigidity left his body, his shoulders relaxing beneath the light blue cotton polo shirt he wore. "I'm not an expert but I don't think a person's basic characteristics change. They might pretend, but after a while their true self shines through. You're a good person, Kiran. I wish you'd accept that. Besides, what happens if your memory never returns? Are you going to go through life terrified to take chances because of a past you don't remember?"

"It's easy for you. You're not the one with the problem."

Rohan placed his hand on Kiran's shoulder. "This is getting old. I want you, both the good and the bad. For God's sake, no one is perfect. I'm no prize. You should hear Ambar detail my many faults. I don't want perfect. I want you." His gaze was earnest, full of pleading. "Please, Kiran. I've never responded to another person, male or female like I do with you. Can't you give us a chance?" His golden-brown eyes beseeched Kiran, adding to the power emanating from his words.

How could Kiran resist?

"Yes." Kiran broke into a smile, bursting with pleasure inside, with belonging, and for once the dark chasm of the past didn't seem insurmountable. He had people here in Middlemarch, people who cared about him. He felt useful, maybe even loved. He dragged in a deep breath, his nose wrinkling at the fragrant scent of cow manure. Retracing his steps, he toed off his boots and peeled off his socks, leaving them both at the door. "I need a shower."

"Is that all you're going to say?"

"Until I have a shower." In the bathroom, Kiran stripped off his borrowed T-shirt and jeans. He reached into the shower and flicked on the water.

The click of the door closing attracted his attention. Rohan stood inside the door, his hands rapidly yanking off his shirt. He removed his sandals and unfastened his jeans without taking his gaze off Kiran. The intensity of Rohan's steady look seared straight through Kiran's body, bringing tension of an entirely different sort. His cock started to lengthen.

"You joining me in the shower?" The husky cadence of Kiran's words gave away his feelings on the subject. Nothing he'd enjoy more.

"Try and stop me." Rohan's grin, the edge of lust and anticipation it contained tightened Kiran's body even more. "Never doubt I want you. I'm not going to push for marking yet, but know I want to claim you. I talked to Saber the other night about the mating process and know how it works now, what to expect. I want you to wear my mark so every other feline knows you belong to me. I'm giving you time to accept me and the life we're gonna lead here in Middlemarch. When you're ready, tell me."

Rohan's certainty was a revelation to Kiran. He didn't think he'd ever had anyone believe in him. Rohan's gaze branded him with love and positive affirmation. Longing surged in him and he shivered, his emotions close to the surface, prickling behind his eyes.

Vulnerable.

He disliked that part of the equation, but he'd already learned to trust Rohan. Both brother and sister bore an innate goodness that shone through despite their strict upbringing. There was none of the resentment Kiran would have expected. They'd loved their parents yet hadn't been blind to their faults. If Rohan could accept his parents' faults, then his words about acceptance meant something.

But Kiran still stressed, still held fear close to his chest.

Swallowing his nerves, Kiran stepped under the water, standing to the side to allow Rohan room to enter. His lover moved into the gap and closed the shower door, confining them in a private world. Kiran picked up the soap and lathered his hands.

Rohan grabbed the bar of soap from him and rubbed it across Kiran's chest. "Let me get rid of the animal scent first then we're gonna have some fun. Do you want to take the job with Gavin?"

Kiran nodded. "I like working with you and Ambar, but I'd like to feel as if I'm contributing financially. Every item of clothing I own belongs to you. I want to buy things of my own."

"I can understand that," Rohan said. "Part of the reason Ambar and I decided to move was to start over without our parents' ghosts looking over our shoulders."

"I don't think I'll be earning much, but I liked working outdoors and helping Gavin." He decided not to mention the communication with the animals because he needed to wrap his head around the fact first. "Gavin says I can start as soon as I want."

"You should do it."

"Even if it means working odd hours?"

"I can deal with anything as long as I know you'll return home to me each night," Rohan said.

Silent messages flowed between them. Kiran took in Rohan's broad shoulders, the bulge of his biceps as he stroked the soap over him. Rohan's dark eyelashes looked spiky with the steam and water, delicate fans above his cheeks. Unable to resist, Kiran lifted a hand to trace Rohan's full lips. They looked good stretched around a cock and felt great moving against his own.

Without skipping a beat, Rohan took one of Kiran's fingers into his mouth and sucked hard. Kiran gasped as the sensation echoed in his dick.

"Damn," he whispered on a moan.

Rohan licked his finger and released it with a loud smacking noise.

"You make me hot," Rohan said. "I love touching you, the way you shiver and moan. It's sexy."

The steam from the hot water filled the shower stall, along with the clean scent of citrus soap. Rohan dragged the soap over Kiran's pectoral muscles, rubbing it over his nipples until they hardened to tight nubs. Kiran fought to remain silent, the moan that burst forth bringing a victorious grin from Rohan.

"Score! Turn around and I'll do your back."

Kiran turned slowly, bracing his hands against the top of the stall. The combination of the soap and Rohan's hands sent pleasure humming through his body. Everywhere Rohan touched quivered with sensitivity. His shoulders. The hard knobs of his spine.

"You have a lot of old scars."

"Yeah." Gavin had mentioned his scars. There could be any number of explanations but Kiran's mind kept returning to a whip.

Rohan ran the soap under his armpits. Kiran winced and immediately Rohan drew the soap down a biceps.

"Ticklish, huh?"

"A little," Kiran conceded.

"Handy to know." Rohan's voice held a hint of laughter, and Kiran's mouth curled into a wide smile. He enjoyed being with Rohan like this, the teasing and safety. Rohan moved his attention to Kiran's back again, gradually working down to his ass. Kiran tensed a fraction, anticipating a move into sexual, but Rohan kept the contact clean. How he managed to keep hold of the soap bemused Kiran. He struggled to retain the thought. Rohan's gliding hands took precedence and his mind wandered into the future.

This was how it could be between them. Laughter. Pleasure. Love.

Damn, he was a fool to even think about walking away. Rohan was right about living in the here and now, looking to the future, but something inside him refused to blow off his fears. Rohan's fingers crept between the globes of his ass, tickling across his entrance before retreating, moving between his legs to his balls. A slow twist of Rohan's wrist slid the soap across his scrotum.

More, Kiran thought. Damn, that felt good. His cock strained, and Kiran's hands tightened on the top of the stall.

"Widen your stance for me," Rohan ordered.

Kiran didn't consider objecting. He spread his legs and waited, his stomach bucking at the thought of what Rohan might do next. He wanted more direct touching yet the drag of the soap across his skin and the firm press of Rohan's fingers sent his eagerness soaring, a moan of enjoyment building in his chest.

The soap ran over his butt, a finger pressing his perineum briefly before moving away. His cock jerked, the rush of excitement from sensitive nerve endings beating at his willpower. He could always turn and attack, make Rohan drop the soap and get to the good stuff faster. Kiran didn't do that. Instead he suffered through the pleasure.

Rohan ran the soap across the sensitive skin of his inner thighs, tantalizingly close before retreating to skim across the muscles and tendons of his legs and calves. His feet.

Then, the hand lifted from his body. He sensed Rohan standing behind him and knew he was right when the soap splattered into the tiny puddle of water that had collected in the soap dish.

"Turn around." Rohan's voice emerged low and husky, taut with lust.

Kiran suppressed a shudder, moving purposely slow just to hear Rohan's voice again.

"Turn around," Rohan repeated, and Kiran released his grip on the top of the stall to turn to face him.

Rohan's brows rose when he saw the poorly hidden grin on Kiran's face.

"You did that on purpose."

"You're so sexy when you rasp out orders. It makes me hot." Kiran's smile widened when he noticed the sexy glitter in Rohan's eyes. He noticed something else too. "You want me."

"Of course I do. That's a given," Rohan said. "You talk too much. Stop."

Kiran snorted. "Make me."

"My pleasure." He crowded Kiran into the corner of the shower and took possession of his mouth. He ate at Kiran's lips with an air of desperation, nipping his bottom lip before laving the sting away. Their tongues slid together in a sensuous dance. Rohan's fingers slipped into his hair and he held him tight, mastering him with the kiss, fueling his need.

Kiran closed his eyes and immediately slipped into a series of flickering pictures. Blood. Damn, there was so much blood, yet the master held his head and wouldn't let him move. Bubbling sounds of horror came from deep in his chest, yet the dying woman still kissed him, still dripped blood over his face. With a burst of strength, he ripped from his captor's touch, a yell of fear echoing around him.

"Kiran? Kiran!"

Kiran's eyes blinked open to find Rohan studying him with a worried expression on his face.

There was no blood. No dead woman.

Kiran swallowed and bit his bottom lip to stop the unmanly quiver. "I...I don't think I like my head being held like that. I...damn!" He swiped his hands over his eyes, trying to block out the concern in Rohan's face. "I...can we talk about this later?"

"Of course," Rohan said. "It's just your head?"

"Yeah, I know you've done that to me before and I didn't freak but...fuck! I'm sorry."

"You have no need to apologize. How about something to take your mind off your flashback?"

Flashback.

Yeah, that's exactly what he'd had. It had felt so real and connected with his other dreams so well that he knew the memory held an element of truth. He coughed to clear his throat and nodded, striving for lightness. "What did you have in mind?"

"Why don't you wait and see?" When Kiran hesitated, Rohan said, "If something bothers you then tell me. The last thing I want to do is to make you afraid."

This time Kiran nodded, and with a confident grin, Rohan knelt in front of him. He grasped his thighs for balance and started to explore his genitals. The tension bled from Kiran in one harsh exhalation when Rohan's hand curled around his shaft. A moan built as Rohan pumped it hard in the way Kiran loved. He gripped him in an uncompromising fist with no tentativeness. Perfect. It felt bloody perfect, and soon the tension humming through his body was the good kind.

When Rohan released his dick, he nearly complained, but almost instantly a warm, hot mouth surrounded his tip. Gentle fingers stroked and probed his balls, the sensation becoming gradually firmer and more forceful, almost to the point of pain.

"Damn that feels good," Kiran said in a guttural voice.

Rohan didn't speak but glanced up to meet his gaze. Everything he felt showed in his eyes—the love, the acceptance. The pleasure he felt.

Hesitantly, Kiran ran his fingers over Rohan's dark hair, and his lover smiled around his shaft, silently encouraging him, telling him he could take a bit of force. Rohan sucked his cock, letting the underside rub along his tongue. Kiran tried not to move. Success was short-lived, and his hips jerked, driving his cock deeper into Rohan's mouth. His legs quivered under the sensual onslaught, the pleasure a river of sensations, one running into the next until he groaned aloud. The tension built with each suck, each painful tug of his balls. He fought, struggling to make it last, but eventually the stimulation became too much for him. Kiran shattered with a heartfelt groan of delight, his entire body shuddering in reaction.

Gradually he came back to his senses and realized the water pouring over their heads had become frigid, and Ambar would be pissed. He grinned at the thought as he helped Rohan stand. Pulling him into his embrace, he said, "Ambar's gonna shout at you for using all the hot water."

"Huh," Rohan said. "If you think I'm taking the blame on my own you have rocks in your head."

Kiran ignored the cold water to kiss Rohan, pouring every emerging feeling into the intimate contact. Rohan was a hard man to ignore. Kiran didn't want to fight the battle anymore. Rohan was right. They'd celebrate the future and let the past take care of itself.

They were both breathing hard when they pulled apart. Kiran flipped off the water and went to sink to his knees.

"Hold that thought for later. I promised Ambar I'd do dinner tonight."

"Are you sure?"

"I sucked you off because I wanted to. I don't expect anything in return." Rohan winked. "Not right now anyway."

CHAPTER SIX

"I'M LOOKING FORWARD TO this run," Ambar said, leaning between the front seats to speak to Kiran and Rohan. "I would have enjoyed it with just us, but to run with Saber and Gavin and Leticia is exciting. I wonder if Charlie and Emily feel left out. I know I would."

Rohan shot a glance at Kiran, concerned by his silence. While Ambar jumped about with excitement, scarcely able to sit still, Kiran had hardly said a word.

"It should be fun," Ambar said. "It's so good not having to worry about nosy people gawking through the windows or running at odd hours and spoiling our fun."

Rohan decided to force a reaction. "Are you looking forward to the run?"

"What if I can't shift?"

"That's silly," Ambar said with a scoffing sound. "Felines don't forget how to shift."

"That's enough, Ambar," Rohan said.

Ambar must have realized her tact had misfired. She pulled a face. "Sorry."

Kiran glanced out the window, pretending interest in the scenery. "I was thinking about shifting before, the mechanics of it, and my mind went blank. I don't know how."

Reaching over, Rohan placed his hand on Kiran's knee and gave it a reassuring squeeze. "It doesn't matter either way." Rohan wanted to offer platitudes and tell Kiran it wouldn't matter to him if he never shifted again or recovered his memory. Gut instinct told him that wouldn't be the right thing to say. If he were the one with no recollection of his past, it would matter to him.

"This must be it." He pulled up and parked, switching off the ignition to leave a heavy silence.

"There they are." Ambar jumped out of the vehicle and hurried over to join Leticia and Emily.

Rohan bent over to snare Kiran's attention. He pressed a kiss to Kiran's lips, keeping it simple but trying to offer comfort and love at the same time. His thoughts staggered at the thought. Yeah, love. That was exactly it. If he had his way, he'd haul Kiran off to a private place and mark him in the blink of an eye. Kiran wasn't ready. It was the only thing that held Rohan back.

"Come on. Let's go." Rohan opened his door and waited. A flash of impatience hit him when Kiran dallied. *Dammit, couldn't he try instead of acting so whipped?*

Through the vehicle window, Rohan saw Kiran's broad chest rise and fall as if he heaved a sigh. He exploded into movement then, bursting out of the SUV. A trace of panic rippled across his face, his cheeks pale. Rohan's impatience fell away, and he found himself rounding the vehicle.

"Kiran?"

Kiran swallowed, his throat moving with the gulp. "I'm scared."

"That's okay." Rohan reached for his hand, feeling pleasure when Kiran's fingers wrapped around his. "Come on. Gavin's here. We'll help, and if you can't shift, it doesn't matter. There's no pressure."

"Easy for you to say."

"Yeah, it is, but I really don't care how this plays out. All I want is to feel you beside me in my bed every night. To feel you inside me."

Kiran sighed. "We don't always get what we want."

Fear shot through Rohan then. It was the hopeless note in Kiran's voice, the acceptance that he didn't deserve happiness. "Let's go." He started walking, dragging Kiran until he followed of his own volition.

Until Kiran had entered his life he hadn't connected with anyone else, he hadn't wanted another man with the intensity he wanted Kiran. Despite Kiran's earlier words and his excitement about his job, he now seemed resigned and depressed. Rohan didn't know what had happened in the interim, but there was no way he intended to let Kiran slip out of his life without a fight. No way.

"Great night for a run," Gavin said when they reached the group.

"Kiran is worried because he doesn't remember how to shift," Ambar blurted.

"Why don't you button up?" Rohan sent Ambar a frustrated glare. Being the center of attention wouldn't exactly help.

Saber frowned, glanced at Gavin. "No problem. It will be like the young ones shifting for the first time. We'll talk you through it."

"They don't always shift the first time, so don't feel pressured," Gavin added.

"Nope, it took me a couple of tries before I shifted for the first time," Leticia said, linking arms with Gavin. "My brother Lucas gave me a hard time because he managed a shift on first attempt."

Her experience didn't relax Kiran any. Rohan felt the tension in his hand and saw it in the strain around his eyes. He tightened his grip until Kiran glanced at him. Rohan forced an encouraging smile and made a mental note to tell Ambar not to tease Kiran about shifting if he failed.

"Emily," Saber said suddenly. "What are you doing with that picnic basket?"

"Carrying it," she said. "I'm pregnant not terminally ill. I can handle a picnic basket."

"Humor him, Emily. Enjoy the pampering while it lasts," Leticia said, wrinkling her nose with an impish grin at her mates.

Despite Emily's protest, she let Saber take the picnic basket. The private smile they shared and the way their gazes both flickered down to Emily's stomach made Rohan feel like a voyeur. And envious. He craved the same closeness in a relationship.

They walked through the gate by a set of cattle yards and made their way across the paddock in twos and threes. There were eight of them including Saber and Emily Mitchell.

"I'm glad we moved to Middlemarch," Rohan said to Kiran. "We're going to be happy here. All of us."

Kiran opened his mouth and closed it again, his shoulders slumping.

"All of us," Rohan repeated. "This is how I shift. I pull up an image of a tiger in my mind and concentrate on it hard. I imagine transforming into the beast and the change starts almost automatically. The first time is hard, and the change hurts. It's a good pain. It brings a high with it, a sense of exhilaration. And when the transformation is complete, it's amazing. You see so much more, smell things you can't in human form. Hear things. You'll see."

Kiran cleared his throat. "Imagining the tiger is part of my problem. The harder I concentrate the worse it is."

"That's easy," Rohan said with a laugh. "I'll change first so you can see me in my tiger form."

Kiran nodded but didn't look confident.

Rohan squeezed his hand, his heart lurching in sympathy. He'd never faced anything like this, changing for the first time with complete self-belief and not a shred of uncertainty. A brash youth at twelve, he'd gone through his first change without incident. Ambar hadn't been much better, shifting with ease for the first time at age thirteen.

Saber and Emily stopped in a sheltered spot in front of a schist outcrop. A gentle breeze bore the scents of grass and the distant herd of cattle. Saber spread a blanket on the ground and settled Emily. Charlie kissed both Leticia and Gavin before dropping to the tussock near Emily.

Rohan noticed Charlie had a daypack. He pulled a soccer ball out and tossed it to Gavin with a grin on his face. "You can play three a side. I'm the referee and my call is final."

Saber whipped off his shirt. "Emily, close your eyes."

An impish grin curled across her lips. "But the scenery is so pretty." She blinked her lashes at him. "I'm a pregnant woman. You should indulge me."

Saber snorted but Rohan saw a softening of his features. He dropped to the blanket at Emily's side. "I'd be happy to indulge you, sweetheart." He leaned over her, pushing her gently back until she sprawled full length on the blanket.

Emily wrinkled her nose. "Spoilsport." But her hands curled around his neck and she returned his kiss with enthusiasm.

Saber lifted his head. "Hurry up and undress while Emily's too busy to watch," he barked out.

"I'll take notes for you, Emily," Charlie said.

Emily giggled. "Appreciate it."

Saber growled and grabbed Emily's attention.

Grinning at the interplay, Rohan started to strip. The others did the same except Kiran and Gavin.

Rohan figured he'd done enough talking. Nothing he'd said so far had convinced Kiran he could shift. He'd go with action. He removed the rest of his clothing and footwear, setting them on a rock.

Closing his eyes, he pictured a tiger in his mind and imagined changing. The familiar prickle shimmered over his skin, giving way to pain as his bones shifted, lengthened. Muscles enlarged, contracted, and Rohan fell forward, vaguely aware of the others shifting around him.

"All done," Charlie said. "You can stop distracting Emily."

"Damn woman will be the death of me," Saber muttered.

"You love me, really." Emily sat up and placed Saber's hand on her stomach. "I have proof."

Saber brushed his fingers over her cheek and rolled to his feet in a fluid move. He removed the last of his clothes and shifted smoothly into a black leopard, padding away to join a lion and a tiger. Rohan waited with Kiran, silently urging him to action, no longer able to speak because of his feline form.

"You okay, Kiran?" Gavin stood at his side, the only feline still in human form.

"Nothing is familiar about doing this. Are you sure I'm a shifter?"

"That's what all my tests say, and Ambar saw you do a partial shift."

Nerves hit Kiran square in the gut. They might think he was a shifter but something told him he had never spent much time in tiger form.

Rohan prowled closer and rubbed his big head against Kiran's thighs. Power emanated from him. Strength. The other man purred, and Kiran stroked his head, sliding his hand over the muscular shoulders and feeling the contrasting softness of his silky fur and firm underlying muscles.

Rohan nudged him roughly before backing up and nailing Kiran with an expectant stare.

Hell.

Gavin placed a hand on his shoulder. "It helps to close your eyes and picture a tiger."

"So everyone keeps telling me." Charlie, Emily and Gavin were all staring at him from where they waited, and Kiran started to feel like an exhibit in a zoo. According to Rohan and Ambar, he'd had a close shave and escaped that terror. He didn't want to make a return. "Stop staring," he ordered.

His words acted as a signal, pushing the others to action. They started to race around the flattish area of tussock in front of where Emily and Charlie sat.

"Why don't you go and join them, Rohan?" Kiran said. "I don't need an audience while I try this."

Rohan hesitated before he glided away across the tussock. Kiran relaxed a fraction when Rohan left, his chest heaving up and down as he exhaled. Pressure to shift intensified the stress. What if he couldn't do this? Although everyone said it didn't matter, he badly wanted to do this. For once he wanted to feel exactly like the others.

"Can I get stuck halfway between feline and human forms?" That would really make him stand out.

Gavin hesitated, and Kiran read the answer in his eyes before he replied. "I've heard of it happening, although I haven't witnessed it in person."

"If that happens is there a cure or is the feline stuck that way?" Kiran wasn't sure he wanted to know the answer for this one.

"I'll admit it's not good," Gavin said.

"Stop trying to stall," Charlie said. "You're making yourself crazy imagining worst-case scenarios."

"I agree with Charlie," Emily said. "Just do it."

All three studied him expectantly.

"The three of you are making me nervous," Kiran said. "Talk about pressure."

"Gavin, shift and go play with the others. Now," Emily ordered.

Charlie smirked at his mate. "You shouldn't mess with a pregnant lady. I'd do what she says if I were you."

Kiran thought that sounded like a fine idea. "I'll call you if I need you. And if I can't call you either Charlie or Emily will do it for me."

Gavin stripped down and shifted. Kiran watched the process carefully, thinking it looked painful. When he turned back to Charlie and Emily, he noticed Charlie had his fingers over Emily's eyes.

"Saber doesn't like her peeking. He gets a mite testy on the subject," Charlie said.

"Party pooper," Emily said, peeling Charlie's fingers away from her eyes. "Right," she said. "Kiran, strip off and try shifting."

Charlie wagged his finger at her, his mouth quirking with humor. "Don't fall for it, Kiran. She wants to tell Saber she saw you without your clothes."

"I'm gonna tell Saber you were awful to me. I'm a pregnant lady, you know."

"Saber should put you over his knee and spank your butt," Charlie retorted. "Kiran, this is my suggestion. Walk over to that pile of rocks over there and try shifting on your own with no one watching. That way you should be able to concentrate."

Like one of Ambar's curries cooking on the stovetop, nerves bubbled in the pit of Kiran's stomach. Fear he'd fail. That's what it was. Fear he'd disappoint Rohan and his new friends. Dipping his head in a clipped nod, he headed for the rocks. Before he attempted a shift, he glanced across the tussock land to watch the other felines playing. They mock charged, leapt on each other and playful growls filled the air along with Charlie and Emily's chatter and laughter. They were a tight-knit bunch and they'd extended the hand of friendship to him. He had to do this. He had to shift.

Slowly he removed his footwear and clothing, placing them in a neat pile. His palms grew clammy, his breathing choppy.

"Damn," he whispered.

He rubbed his palms over his thighs and inhaled deep until his lungs expanded and some of his fear receded. Gradually he let the air ease out, and while the fear remained, it was manageable. When he peeked from behind the rock, he saw Rohan and Ambar galloping around with the others. His gaze stroked Rohan's body, memorizing the other man's musculature. Closing his eyes, he pictured the body he'd committed to memory and concentrated hard.

Nothing happened.

His shoulders slumped and a raft of goose bumps prickled across his flesh.

He'd failed.

The need to run with the others prodded him. Disappointment. Rohan and the others wouldn't think less of him for his inability to shift. That knowledge didn't matter.

He felt the lack inside, felt like half a man.

Swallowing, he decided to try again. This time it seemed more natural to call up the feline in his mind. The brownish-orange coat with black stripes. He frowned and instinctively altered the color. Heat prickled over his skin, akin to a mild shock. He gasped, the pain taking him by surprise. Fur rippled over his skin and claws pushed from beneath his finger and toenails. His gums burned as canines pushed upward.

A groan squeezed from between his clenched lips, the sound barely human. He dropped to his hands and knees, the ripple of pain now tinged with satisfaction—delight—as his bones rippled and reformed. Then, it was over and every sense screamed with pleasure. His sight. His hearing.

He padded from behind the rock and ambled over to Emily and Charlie.

"Oh my," Emily said, her mouth curling into a wide smile. "Aren't you pretty?"

"A white tiger," Charlie said. "From what I hear they're rare."

Elated by his successful shift, Kiran rubbed his head against Charlie's shoulder and did the same to Emily, tempering his strength with her.

Laughing, she rubbed her hand over his shoulder. "Go and play with the others. Charlie and I will sort out teams in a moment."

Kiran scampered out to join the others, savoring the myriad scents and the feel of the dry tussock beneath his paws. When he neared Rohan he slowed, making a low sound like a quick rush of air combined with a rumble. Rohan swung around, stared for an instant then chuffled in return. Seconds later he rubbed his head against Kiran in a show of welcome and contentment.

One at a time the shifters greeted him, rubbing and scenting Kiran. Exhilarated and excited, Kiran stood his ground and let them brush against him.

Charlie interrupted them. "Teams. Saber, Rohan and Leticia against Gavin, Kiran and Ambar. When you're ready, I'll toss the ball in. Saber's team—your goal is between those two rocks there." He gestured with his hand. "Gavin's team—your goal is between that flat rock and the scrubby bush. Okay?"

Saber let out a sharp growl and Gavin followed suit. Bemused, Kiran followed Gavin and Ambar. Kiran had never played a game like this before and he didn't know what to do.

His soft grunt attracted Gavin's attention. *What do I do?* He sent his thought soaring toward Gavin, wanting answers so he didn't make a fool of himself.

Kiran?

Yeah. I don't know how to play this game. What do I do?

You communicate. Gavin sounded shocked, and Kiran caught his quick glance at Saber and his team. *Can you communicate with Ambar?*

I don't know. Should I try?

Hell, yeah! Gavin's lip turned up, reminding Kiran of a human smirk.

Ambar? Can you hear me? Gavin wants to know.

Holy shit! She stared at him, her whiskers twitching. *You can mind speak? Why didn't you tell us? I've never heard of anyone doing that before. You're a white tiger. Why didn't we know you were white? I'm sure they didn't mention it on the news.*

Kiran made a low rumbling sound. *Gavin, is this unusual? Weird?*

We are gonna whip their asses. Kiran, Ambar and I can't communicate, and I couldn't hear her talking to you. It seems to me that you initiate the conversation and that shifter can communicate back. We'll discuss it later. We'll fan out in a line with you in the middle. I want you to keep communicating with us while we play the ball. They don't have the advantage of knowing what their team members are going to do. Gavin rubbed his nose over Kiran's face. *Experiment. See if you can overhear the others without letting them know you can talk back.*

Ambar let out a soft chuffle, layered with inquiry. Kiran told her their plan and with a nod she trotted away. He and Gavin turned to face the others.

Charlie stood on the sideline. "I'm throwing the ball in now. No teeth because this is the only ball we have. And remember Emily and I are the ones with the power. Our word is law."

The white ball sailed through the air, landing exactly in the middle of the two opposing teams. There was a second's hesitation before each shifter sprang into motion.

Mock growls and rumbles filled the air, the sounds different from each type of shifter. Kiran threw himself into the melee. The ball bounced near Leticia and she bounded after it, batting it with her head and controlling it with her front paws. With a thump of a paw, she sent the ball rolling toward Saber. The ball hit a rock, throwing it off course. Ambar dived on it.

Pass it to Gavin. Kiran inserted himself between Ambar and Leticia, giving Ambar time to pass to Gavin. *Gavin, ball coming your way. Ambar, sneak off to the right so Gavin can pass it to you to score.*

The strategy worked perfectly, their adept passing and decoys from Kiran taking Saber's team by surprise. Ambar hit the ball with her with her front paws and it sailed between the rock and scrubby tree.

"One-nil to Gavin's team," Charlie shouted.

Despite their advantage, the score seesawed between the two teams. The light faded, but it didn't slow the shifters down. Kiran didn't overhear any of the others thinking, and he could only hear Gavin and Ambar if he initiated the conversation.

"Last throw in," Charlie called. "Emily and I can't see very well now."

This one is ours. Kiran communicated their play, and they burst into action. Saber and his team were more aware of their strategies of passing now and marked their opposites closely.

Ambar had the ball and, with Rohan about to tackle her for possession, Kiran decided they needed an edge.

Get ready to receive the ball from Ambar. Ambar, pass the ball to Gavin then block so they can't get to him.

As Kiran suspected, Rohan tackled his sister, hoping to manhandle her so Saber could sneak the ball.

Rohan, don't get too tired. You're gonna fuck me tonight, and it will be fantastic. Saber, Emily needs you right now! Ambar, go! Pass the ball to Gavin. Gavin, the ball is coming your way.

While Saber and Rohan paused in confusion, Kiran and Gavin completed the sneaky maneuver, scoring the goal before Saber and his teammates had a chance to recover.

Charlie waved his arms above his head. "Score! Game to Gavin and his team. Losers buy drinks for us and chocolate for Emily."

"*Ooh* yes," Emily said. "Chocolate, peanut butter and banana sandwiches. That's what I feel like for supper."

Saber shifted and stalked over to Emily. "Your wish is my command. Close your eyes while the others shift and dress."

Emily laughed and obediently closed her eyes. "One day, Saber, I'm going to manage to see. What's so weird about the rest of them? Do they have two cocks or an extra nipple?"

Charlie snorted with amusement, but Kiran watched him eye his partners as they shifted, sexual interest gleaming in his eyes.

Saber kissed Emily on the forehead, the expression on his face full of tenderness. "I like you looking at me. You don't need to look at the others."

"Way to go, Kiran," Gavin said in an undertone. "I didn't realize you were a white tiger. We'll talk at work tomorrow. You are going to work with me, right?"

"I didn't realize I was a white tiger either. I think that's why I had problems shifting. I was visualizing the wrong thing." Kiran paused before heading to where he'd left his clothes. "I'd really like to take the job with you."

"Good. Eight tomorrow morning at the surgery."

Kiran nodded. For the first time in a long time, Kiran felt as if he were part of the community. He felt as if he mattered.

Fully dressed, he joined the others as they made their way back to the vehicles.

"We'll see you at our place shortly," Emily said.

Kiran joined Rohan and Ambar in their vehicle.

"Neat party trick," Ambar said, hugging Kiran with exuberance. "I still can't believe you're a white tiger. Why didn't they mention that on the news?"

"Maybe they did mention he was white and we missed it. We only caught the headlines. What party trick? What are you talking about?" Rohan glanced from one to the other, his brow puckered in confusion.

Ambar's brows rose and she grinned but didn't say anything.

Kiran turned to Rohan. "It seems I can communicate with others while in tiger form."

"You? That was you talking to me earlier?" Rohan's voice held astonishment and a touch of chagrin. "You purposely distracted me."

"I distracted Saber too," Kiran admitted with a grin. "It was easy."

Rohan and Ambar stared at him, identical expressions of wonder on their faces.

"Do you realize how rare that is? Being able to do that?" Rohan asked. "I don't think I've ever heard of anyone communicating like that."

"Yeah," Ambar piped in. "Not only are you a white tiger, which is rare to start with, you have a *woo-woo* factor going on as well." She held up her hands and wriggled all her fingers in illustration.

Kiran's mouth dropped open. "*Woo-woo?* That makes me sound freaky."

"Not freaky." Rohan started up the SUV and did a three-point turn. "You're extraordinary. Unique." His eyes blazed with sudden heat. "Very sexy."

"What did Gavin say?" Ambar asked.

"We're going to talk about it tomorrow when I start my new job."

Rohan reached out to grasp his knee and squeezed. "I'm so proud of you."

"I'm so glad we came to Middlemarch," Ambar said. "That was fun. I can't wait to do it again." She grasped Kiran's shoulder, pausing a fraction when he started. "Sorry, I didn't mean to startle you. I wanted to say I'm on your team. Once we refine the communication, we'll be a force to reckon with." Glee shaded her tone, the sly glance she sent toward Rohan making Kiran want to chuckle. Their sibling rivalry cracked him up, and even better, he liked the way they included him in their discussions.

He prayed that never changed.

LATER THAT NIGHT, KIRAN and Rohan didn't even pretend to go to their separate rooms. They both said goodnight to Ambar and Kiran followed Rohan to his room. The door closed behind them, leaving them privacy.

"You are gorgeous." Rohan stalked him, pushing Kiran into the wall when their chests brushed. He brushed a lock of hair from Kiran's face, searching deep into his eyes. Kiran didn't bother trying to suppress his reactions, letting his emotions show without censorship. With Rohan, it seemed right and natural.

Rohan followed the path of his fingers with his mouth. "You taste of the outdoors. Smell of it too."

"It was great tonight."

"I told you it would be okay," Rohan said.

"I thought a shift might have helped with my memory. It hasn't."

"How many times do I have to tell you? I don't care about your past. It's your future I'm interested in." Rohan unfastened the buttons on Kiran's shirt and peeled it back to expose his chest. "Gorgeous. Sexy. Perfect."

Their clothes and footwear melted away and they moved to the bed.

"So I'm gonna fuck you tonight," Rohan said. "That's what you think?"

A faint tinge of color collected in Kiran's cheeks. Heat and hope surged to the fore. "That's what I anticpate will happen." He hoped with every particle of his body, wanting to show his feelings for Rohan in the earthiest way possible.

"You're not going to make excuses about the possible horrors in your past?"

"No. I'll admit the big chunk of emptiness frightens me, but I don't want to focus on it any longer. I want to concentrate on us."

Rohan crawled over Kiran's naked body until he smiled down at him. "I like the way you think." He settled his weight on Kiran and explored his mouth.

Even though they'd fooled around before, this time seemed more real. A world of color instead of black and white. Kiran let his tongue twirl with Rohan's, tasting the other shifter and participating in the kiss. Their breathing became harsher, their cocks harder, the sensations tumbling through him more demanding.

Rohan's hands were everywhere. Tugging at Kiran's hair, pinching his nipples. Rohan kissed his mouth, the in-and-out flicker of his tongue dragging a groan from Kiran.

"Do you think you need much preparation to take me?"

Kiran thought about the dreams. "I don't think so."

Rohan didn't ask why. "I'll take things slow. It never hurts to use plenty of lube." He stroked Kiran's shaft, brushing his finger over the sensitive head while dipping his tongue into Kiran's bellybutton.

A shot of pleasure zigzagged through his lower belly, striking his balls. His breath exploded from him in a hoarse exhalation. He shivered, arching up into Rohan's touch.

"Feel good?" Humor shaded Rohan's voice.

"Real good. Do it again. Please."

Rohan repeated the move, the blast of pleasure making Kiran groan. Then Rohan's mouth settled over the head of his cock. Kiran shuddered, the hit of extra warmth curling his toes. He felt the slide of Rohan's finger across taut balls, the gentle handling and exploration before Rohan moved on to explore another part of his body.

"You make me feel so needy, Rohan. I want this, I want you."

Rohan made a humming sound of approval around Kiran's cock and ran a finger down his perineum. The firm stepping motion of his fingers combined with the suction of Rohan's mouth made Kiran writhe, made him impatient. The finger circled his rosette, delicately stimulating nerves, firing his balls until he thought he might come before they reached the truly good stuff.

A single finger probed him, the stretch of tight muscles bringing a pleasurable burn. If he felt this way now, how would he feel with Rohan inside him? Damn, he couldn't wait.

"Please go faster," he said with a hint of demand. "Rohan, I need you to take me. Claim me," he added, flushing at the implication of his words. His words gave Rohan power. In his dreams, he was the powerless one. He'd felt both weak and degraded, yet now he was willingly giving himself over to Rohan.

"Nothing I'd like better," Rohan replied in a husky voice.

Emotion, it shimmered between them. A step forward to a partnership. That's what it felt like to Kiran and his heart rejoiced in their closeness, not a shred of fear in evidence.

They kissed, lips moving in a teasing tango, brush and retreat, flirtation before deepening to intense and bold. A silent exchange of promises, the moment tender and full of passion and fire. Rohan wriggled his finger a little before removing it.

Kiran made a protest against Rohan's mouth. Rohan lifted his head and grinned. "Don't panic. I'm gonna grab the lube. I don't want to hurt you. Any pain should be the good sort that makes your balls go tight and your toes curl. That's the only pain either of us should have to suffer through."

The care in Rohan loosened a tight band from around Kiran's chest, something rooted in the past that he didn't recall at the moment. All he knew was Rohan's consideration eased something inside him.

"Luckily, I'd hoped to need the lube in the near future so I have some handy in the drawer."

"I'm all for preplanning." Kiran ran a hand over Rohan's back as he leaned over to open the top drawer of the heavy bedside cabinet.

"Do you want to use condoms? I haven't been with anyone for over a year. There hasn't been time."

"No condoms," Kiran said. "Gavin tested me for FIV and said I'm clear. He said that's the only thing we need to worry about."

"I know. I was there, remember? Maybe I should have asked him to test me as well." Scowling, he plucked a condom from the drawer along with the bottle of lube. "We're not risking it. I'll ask him to test me tomorrow."

Kiran nodded, despite wanting to argue the point. The truth—they had plenty of time. His test hadn't taken long since Gavin's surgery was set up to service the feline community. Rohan's test wouldn't be equally quick and would set both their minds at rest.

Rohan tucked the condom under the pillow and flipped the lid on the lube, squirting a dollop onto his fingers. He kissed Kiran, firing the caress with passion and heat. Kiran gasped, and Rohan slipped his tongue into Kiran's mouth, stroking with clear intent. Kiran's heart beat faster and his need escalated. He stirred restlessly, groaning when the head of his cock slid along Rohan's hip in a sizzling stroke. His hips jerked, trying to repeat the move, but Rohan laughed and dodged.

"Hold that thought," he said. "Spread your legs for me. Yeah. Like that." Rohan rubbed a finger over his entrance, then pushed a lubed finger inside. A second finger followed shortly afterward, scissoring open to stretch Kiran.

"The lube is cold."

"You're welcome to fuck me any time you want," Rohan said, silent promises in his eyes but no apologies.

"I'll bear that in mind." Kiran let his eyes close and concentrated on the intrusion of Rohan's fingers, the sweet burn of pain and pleasure. The stretch. He let his mind wander, abuzz with sensation. When Rohan mentioned him having a turn, the idea had seemed foreign. He didn't know if he'd done it before or not.

Rohan slid his fingers deep, angling them to slither across Kiran's gland. Rohan watched his lover's face and knew the exact moment when he did it right. Kiran gasped, shuddered, his hips bucking. "Good, huh?"

"Yeah."

Kiran's beautiful blue-green eyes stared at him with something akin to shock. It made Rohan wonder about his past. Part of him wanted Kiran to remember so he had answers and the other part worried about the past. All the small signs indicated a hard life and maybe abuse. The idea of someone hurting Kiran irked Rohan.

He slid his fingers deep, taking pleasure in making Kiran feel good. His own cock was so damn tight he thought he might explode any minute. Kiran didn't look in much better shape. After another pump of his fingers, he pulled free and grabbed the condom. In seconds flat he rolled it onto his cock. After adding more lube, he lined up and pushed into Kiran's searing heat. Rohan watched Kiran's face the entire time, holding in place until he was sure he wasn't hurting him.

"You're not hurting me," Kiran said, reading his mind. "The only way you'll do that is if you don't hurry."

Rohan barked out a laugh, pulled back and pushed deeper this time. The tight grip of Kiran's channel made him grimace. "Going slow won't be a problem." As if to prove his statement, he withdrew and thrust. Kiran echoed his groan. Rohan pulled back and this time slid home. Kiran gripped his shoulders and pulsed around Rohan's cock. It was intimate. It was personal. Incredible.

A tremble slipped through Rohan, his arms shaking as he braced them on either side of Kiran's body. He wanted to prolong their encounter. He wanted to go slow and couldn't. Even as the thoughts screamed through his head, he pulled back and slid deep again, setting up a rhythm. Increasingly faster, his strokes no longer measured but choppy. Jerky and verging on loss of control.

Kiran let out a needy sound, not far short of a whimper. Rohan wanted to grip Kiran's cock and drive him to the point of insanity with his hands, except that would mean he'd have to stop the driving thrusts.

"Touch yourself, Kiran."

Kiran blinked, and Rohan sensed he'd never considered the idea. Maybe because of his past conditioning. Rohan made a silent vow to make sure Kiran knew they were a partnership, that nothing they wanted or did together was wrong or dirty.

He attempted to slow and repositioned his body so his cock slid in at a different angle. Kiran's surprised hiss told him he'd managed to get it right.

"Rohan," he muttered, his voice strained. "I can't hold back, not if I touch myself. Sorry."

"I'm not asking you to hold back. This isn't a competition between us. We don't have to come together." Rohan slowed his strokes even though it almost killed him. Gritting his teeth didn't help. "This is about pleasure, about giving and taking. It's about us. Whatever we decide is what's right." He withdrew and paused with only the head of his cock inside Kiran. "Okay?" The sharp spasm of Kiran's rectum around the tip of his dick made him hiss with pleasure, but he wanted to make a point. Kiran had to stop reacting to his past conditioning. It bothered him even though Kiran didn't realize he was doing it. "*Okay?*"

"Yeah. Don't stop!" A panicked look filled Kiran's expression, along with worry. He gnawed his bottom lip.

"I'm not gonna stop. I promise." This was obviously going to take time and trust. He made a mental note to talk with Gavin. "It would kill me to stop."

"Good. That's good." Kiran gnawed his lip again, scanned Rohan's face, and must have felt reassured by what he saw. He grasped his shaft, stroking it with a firm grip.

"Yeah, it is good," Rohan said, sliding home. This time he gave in to the lure of pleasure, surrendering even as he angled his strokes to pass the feel-good sensations on to Kiran. If he'd thought his balls were tight before, he was wrong. Each stroke intensified the feeling, making it worse, his need more demanding. The scent of sex and arousal filled the air.

Kiran gave a loud groan and semen splashed against his fingers and chest. His channel clenched around Rohan's cock. Rohan gave one last hard, digging stroke and came with a soft curse. When the spasms died down, he fell against Kiran. Kiran's arms came around Rohan, holding him tight, and it felt as if he were home.

CHAPTER SEVEN

"Hey, lover. It's morning. We need to get out of bed before Ambar comes looking for us." Rohan laughed when Kiran wrinkled his nose.

"I get the feeling it wouldn't embarrass her."

"Nope. The best we can do is take notes and give her a hard time when she starts dating." Unable to deny himself, Rohan leaned closer to kiss Kiran. Their lips slid together as if they'd been partners for a long time. The comfortable feeling swelled his heart with a blaze of happiness. The kiss between them swiftly morphed into urgent, cocks swelling with need.

A thump on their bedroom door brought them back to reality. "Hurry up. Coffee is ready and I'm hungry. I'm cooking bacon, eggs, and baked beans this morning. If you want some you need to be in the kitchen in ten minutes." Ambar paused and knocked on the door again. "There's no time for morning nookie."

"Our parents will turn in their graves," Rohan said.

"Newsflash," Ambar retorted through the closed door. "They're already spinning. They've probably disowned us and claimed some other poor kids to haunt." A quick skip of steps indicated Ambar's retreat to the kitchen.

"I think we'll have fun when it's our turn," Kiran said.

Rohan stole another quick kiss on principle before he slid from the bed. The scent of sex, musky bodies, and the splash of dried semen on his belly brought satisfaction. He padded into the bathroom and flipped on the shower. When the water ran warm, he stepped into the cubicle and grabbed the soap.

He noticed a flash of movement and turned a fraction, taking pleasure in observing Kiran. His lover stretched and slipped one hand behind his head to itch the back of his neck, muscles flexing with the sensual move.

"I would invite you to share the shower, but I'm thinking we'd get distracted," Rohan called above the splash of the water.

Kiran's grin was pure sunshine. He leaned against the bathroom cabinet, his gaze skimming Rohan's body. Rohan fumbled the soap and dropped it with a curse. Kiran's chuckle warmed him inside. His cock filled and lengthened, but aware of the passing time and the gnawing ache of hunger in his belly, Rohan hurried through his shower. Kiran handed him a towel and took his place under the warm water.

Back in the bedroom, Rohan dressed in jeans and one of the polo shirts he and Ambar had purchased to wear in the store. They'd decided to keep their shirts uniform and wear jeans or shorts as the season dictated. None of the strict black and white uniforms his parents had insisted they wear whenever they worked in the store.

"Not bad," Ambar said when he joined her in the kitchen. "I thought I'd have to shout through the door again.

Rohan grabbed two cups and poured coffee. "Do you want a refill?" The scent of cooking bacon made his stomach rumble a complaint.

"Please." Ambar stirred the pot of baked beans and jiggled the pan. "Grab some plates, will you? And put on some toast."

Rohan pulled three plates from the cupboard and handed them to Ambar. She served the bacon and eggs and added generous servings of baked beans. They worked together like a well-oiled machine. By the time the coffee and food was on the table, the toast had popped up.

Kiran arrived in a wave of citrus, dressed in one of Rohan's old T-shirts and a pair of the jeans they'd purchased in Dunedin at the same time they'd picked up their new vehicle. He'd put on weight and looked good enough to eat. Maybe even bite, Rohan thought with a twist of his lips.

"Hungry?" Ambar asked.

Kiran nodded. "Yeah, it was the run last night."

"Or it could have been something else," Rohan said, exchanging an intimate look with Kiran.

"*Eew*," Ambar said, wrinkling her nose. "Just *eew*. I'm too young to know about your sex life."

"Yet you want one of your own," Rohan pointed out.

Kiran grinned and applied himself to breakfast. "Thanks for doing breakfast, Ambar. I know it was my turn."

Rohan thought Kiran appeared relaxed and happy, and it delighted him. Kiran was a changed man from when they'd first discovered him in the hospital. The weight gain looked good on him.

"That's all right," Ambar said. "I was awake. You take my turn tomorrow."

"Probably safer for you to do it," Rohan said. "Kiran doesn't seem to be a very good cook."

"That's no excuse," Ambar said. "He'll learn. He is learning."

"Both of you can stop talking like I'm not here." Kiran paused to scratch the back of his neck and smiled. "If you have time today write me an instruction sheet for cooking breakfast for tomorrow. I can follow instructions."

They finished breakfast. Kiran helped Rohan with the dishes and cleaning the kitchen.

"Okay, I'm off to work," Kiran said, and it was easy to see the pride in him. "I'm not sure what time I'll be back. Gavin said it depends on emergencies. I'll ring if I'm gonna be late."

"I'll walk over with you, and see if Gavin has time to do a test for me," Rohan said.

Ambar's brows rose. "Do I want to know?"

"No," Kiran said.

"No!" Rohan shouted at almost the same time.

A smirk formed on Ambar's face. "I'll take that as a no, then." And she calmly picked up the key for the store and left them to it.

DAVID WAS A FOOL. Nando Marsters had observed his oldest brother over the years, taken note. There was so much money to make, yet his brother kept to mainly legal activities. Of course his personal life didn't run with the same aboveboard preciseness. Where sex was concerned David was both bi-sexual and kinky and wasn't afraid to pay for his perversions.

Nando stepped up to the immigration counter and presented his passport. He juggled his duty-free purchase of good Scottish whisky and his laptop from his right hand to his left and smiled. "Good morning."

"Good morning," the customs officer said. "You're here for a holiday?"

"No, business, although if things go well I might take a week and go down to Queenstown. I've always wanted to try bungee jumping in the gorge. You know, the original site."

"Rather you than me. Where are you staying?"

"The Fawkner Hotel in central Auckland," Nando said.

The customs officer nodded and stamped his passport. "Welcome to New Zealand. Keep the agricultural declaration form and hand it in before you exit airport security."

"Thanks." Nando collected his passport and put it in his suit jacket pocket. He strolled through to the luggage collection area. The other passengers scurried around like busy ants. Over to his left, a toddler screamed and dropped to the ground, kicking her feet and beating her tiny fists on the ground. Nando suppressed a shudder.

Like him, others stared at the spectacle. A young pregnant woman who appeared ready to drop her child at any moment rubbed her straining belly. Nando turned away, striding to the other side of the baggage carousel. Pregnant women were disgusting. He didn't like to look at them. When he married he would banish his wife once she became pregnant. She could return to his side once the child came. He liked his women to focus on him, on his needs. He intended to rule his household. He would protect his women, both wife and mistresses, to the best of his ability, and in return, they would treat him like a royal king.

The luggage carousel jerked in a metallic shriek. Bags started appearing and soon Nando spied his. The benefits of flying business class.

At the rental car counter, he presented his gold card and after minimal paperwork, he received a set of keys.

Kiran Ramji had sealed his fate when he'd eavesdropped on business he had no right overhearing. Once Nando realized Kiran had witnessed the murders, that was it. The slave had signed his death warrant. He'd instructed two of the men loyal to him to kill Kiran and get rid of the body. A snarl emerged as he thought of the mess his men had made when they'd disobeyed his orders, compelled by greed. Fortunately, Nando had a second chance to get rid of Kiran.

This time he wouldn't fail. He'd do the job himself.

Nando knew his other brothers would cover for him because he terrified them. They'd made the mistake of thinking the youngest brother should inhabit the lowest rung on the family hierarchy. He'd set them straight with a swift show of violence. A favorite mistress had died at his hands, his team of well-trained bodyguards backing him with silent might. It hadn't taken long for him to exert his power, although he'd taken care to present a different face to David.

Nando respected David. He remembered the treats David had given him during his childhood, an act of kindness from a brother many years older than he. Unfortunately, the time had come for him to make a move and seize power from his brother. A matter of economics.

Nando loaded his bag into the rear of his vehicle and strode around to the driver's seat. He slid behind the wheel and set the GPS system. The zoo. Urgency beat at him. He needed to take care of this last loose end to ensure his empire didn't topple.

"A tiger. All this time David kept Kiran's magical powers secret." Nando snorted, shaking his head at the lost opportunities as he pulled out from the parking lot. He would have used the man. He would've made a formidable bodyguard, the ultimate burglar, but no. His older brother had loved the man, protected his secrets.

Love made a person weak. Nando had learned that at an early age, watching his mother cry when his father disappeared for months and photos appeared in the papers with other women on his arm. Nando signaled a turn, following the directions of the feminine voice coming from the directional system.

Nando found the drive relaxing after the hustle and bustle of India. It was the same whenever he visited a Western country, although he'd never shift his business interests from India. He knew the legal system intimately in his home country, knew who to bribe and how to keep under the radar. No, while he appreciated the Western education he'd received, he liked playing the system in India and using it as his base.

Annoyingly, the zoo crawled with children. He wondered if he should have stopped at his hotel to change into casual clothes so he didn't stand out as much. The last thing he needed was to draw attention. Nando considered the situation and decided to amend his plans. His impatience had almost led him into making a mistake.

Kiran had kept for this long. A few more days meant little because he'd still die.

Death was the only way to clean up this mess.

"HAVE YOU HAD ANY more dreams?" Gavin asked two weeks later.

Kiran shook his head. "Not really. My days are busy now that I work for you and help out at the store."

Gavin glanced over at the only other customers at Storm in a Teacup, took a bite of his ham sandwich, and studied Kiran while he chewed.

"What?" Heat seeped into Kiran's cheeks because of the intensity of Gavin's survey. He scratched the back of his neck and grabbed his juice.

"You seem tired. If I were Emily I'd point out the love bites on your neck."

Kiran almost choked on his mouthful of juice. He swallowed and aimed for calm. "Lucky you're not Emily, then."

A smirk spread across Gavin's face. "Hi, Emily. How are you doing?"

"It depends on who is asking," she said, sliding into the seat Kiran pulled out for her. "If you're gonna fuss like Saber and treat me like a fragile doll, I'm fine. If you're asking as my doctor I have to say I'm feeling a bit tired. It's good to get off my feet. Kiran, what have you and Rohan been doing? I can see two hickeys on your neck. Unless you want to mate you should steer away from the mating site."

Kiran managed a straight face when Gavin smirked at him, even though he wanted to laugh at her lecture. "Rohan and I are making out like rabbits."

"Glad to hear it but take care." Emily switched her attention to Gavin. "Maybe you could mention to Saber that I'm healthy as a horse and just because he's managed to get me pregnant he doesn't need to stop. You might inform him that pregnant women have needs."

Kiran clapped his hands over his ears. "I'm pretty sure an unmated male shouldn't hear that kind of stuff."

Emily reached for his hand and tugged. "Gavin might need a backup. Saber mightn't believe him. I need you to confirm to my husband that I have needs."

"Saber is worried about you," Gavin said. "It's hard for a male to watch his partner go through a pregnancy, but I'll talk to him for you. I want you to take it easy. Leticia would love to help more and feel useful."

"Actually, I've been thinking about adding children's birthday parties to our services, and maybe birthday cakes. Maybe now is a good time to do some planning and costing," Emily said, her eyes narrowing while she thought. "Tomasine and Isabella are always underfoot. I might reorganize the roster and do some planning."

"You could also do special-theme dinners or special nights for Valentine's Day or a midyear Christmas dinner," Gavin said.

"That's a wonderful idea," Emily said, her eyes sparking with enthusiasm. "I have plenty of help. I might have a chat with Ramsay. He's home on holiday now."

"Ramsay stays with Felix and Tomasine," Gavin said to Kiran. "He's training to be a chef."

"Ramsay is going to be a superstar," Emily said. "The boy has talent. Thanks for the suggestions, Gavin. I'll plan a Halloween menu first. Hmm, maybe for a kid's party too. They love scary stuff. Don't forget to talk to Saber." She levered to her feet and, after pausing to speak with the other customers, disappeared into the kitchen.

"Are you going to be popular with Saber?"

Gavin shrugged, his slight grin giving away the fact he wasn't worried. "Probably not, although with a new project Emily might slow down a little. We'll go and see Saber after we're finished here. I know you want to wait, but I think we should tell him about you being able to communicate with animals."

They'd had this conversation a couple of times. "I don't want people to think I'm a freak."

"Hell, I wouldn't employ anyone I considered a freak," Gavin said, his tone a fraction testy. "I don't treat you any differently and neither do Rohan or Ambar. You can trust Saber."

"I'll think about it. I promise."

THEY FOUND SABER AT the cattle yards, the bawl of cattle loud and dust swirling through the air.

"Need a hand?" Gavin asked, leaning out of the SUV window. "Barring an emergency, our next job isn't until two."

"I'm trying to decide which cows to send to the show next month. I'll need to work with them and get them used to handling again," Saber said.

"You want to do your magic?" Gavin asked quietly. "This is a good opportunity. You should let Saber know, if you're intending to stay in Middlemarch."

He wanted to stay. He took a deep breath. "You're right. I'll do it." Kiran felt a glow of belonging and couldn't suppress his grin. "I don't mind Saber knowing, but I wouldn't want it to become public knowledge. I really don't want to become known as the town freak."

"I told you Saber is totally trustworthy. Once he accepts you into his circle, he'll protect you with his life."

Kiran scanned the milling cows and calves, sensed their distinct nervousness. He didn't think it had anything to do with their shifter status since they'd be used to that. "All right. I'll give him a demonstration. That's probably best."

"I can't wait to see this." Gavin climbed out of the SUV and joined Saber.

Kiran wandered over to stand beside them.

"What do you want to do?" Gavin asked.

"It would be good if they'd stand still so I could get a look at each cow and calf and decide which pair has the best chance of winning a ribbon at the show," Saber said, his frustration clear.

Kiran pressed his face against the timber of the yards and peered through the gap. *What's the problem? Why are you so nervous?*

Sending us to abattoir.

No, he's trying to decide which of you will represent the farm at the agricultural show next month. He's hoping some of you will win ribbons.

No death?

No, he's looking for a champion. Can mother and offspring line up together so he can decide who will help him win at the show?

The bawl of the calves halted. The dust settled, and Kiran watched in satisfaction as the animals lined up with the cows at the rear and their calves in front of them. Then he turned to Saber.

"What the hell?" Saber's eyes widened and he rubbed one eye before focusing again.

"Kiran, tell the calves to turn slowly so Saber can see them from the side," Gavin said.

Kiran passed on the instruction and every calf turned and faced the other way.

"Does that help, Saber?" Gavin wasn't very successful in keeping the laughter from his voice.

"You?" Saber turned to nail Kiran with a hard look. "You can communicate with them?"

Kiran took a careful step back before he realized Saber was in total control and didn't intend to hit him. Embarrassment stained his cheeks, and he was glad no one else was present to witness his shame.

"Easy, Saber," Gavin said. "We haven't known for that long. Kiran didn't realize he could communicate with animals. He's been a bit worried about telling people in case they think he's weird. It's hard enough now with him not able to remember his past."

"It might be weird but it's also incredible. Hell, impressive. Just animals?" Saber asked.

Kiran watched him closely. "Animals and shifters when they're in animal form."

Gavin added, "With shifters he can only communicate on a one-to-one basis. They can send thoughts back to him and carry out a conversation, but he can only do that with one shifter at a time. Or that's what we've discovered so far."

"Amazing," Saber said. His eyes narrowed suddenly. "That's how you guys seemed one step ahead of us when we played soccer."

Gavin grinned, and once Kiran decided Saber wasn't going to thump him, he smiled cautiously too.

"Our secret weapon," Gavin said. "He's a natural with animals and his ability to communicate with them speeds things up when we're not sure of a diagnosis. He's turning into a damn fine assistant with both sides of the practice."

Saber picked a piece of grass and chewed on the stalk. "And you still don't remember your past?"

"No. I've had a few dreams that seem real but other than that, I can't remember a thing."

"If you decide to stay in Middlemarch and continue with Gavin, we'll help you with some formal training, if that's what you want," Saber said finally.

"You'd do that for me?" Kiran asked, shock and pleasure combining. He wasn't sure which emotion to allow free range. A lump formed in his throat, and he had to swallow a couple of times before he could even think about speaking again. He scratched the back of his neck, absently noting a sliver of pain. He stopped scratching. "Doesn't it matter about my past?"

"Our pasts shape us," Saber said, "but it's the way we live in the present that men should judge us by, especially if the past is something we can't change. You'll be a real asset to the community."

An asset? "Thank you," Kiran said finally. "Ah, you'd better choose your cattle before they get tired of standing still." He couldn't wait to tell Rohan. Pride filled him now. He felt at home in Middlemarch with both family and friends.

"I can't make up my mind between the cow on the far right and the one second from the left," Saber said.

Kiran instructed them to step forward with their calves and walk the length of the yard and back. Both cows came to a halt in front of Saber and waited.

Saber blinked. "Did you tell them to do that?"

"Yeah." An itch started at the back of Kiran's neck. "Do you want them to do anything else?"

"No. Damn." Saber shook his head. "I'm finding it difficult to get my head around this. You can talk to all animals?"

"Most," Kiran said. "Not birds though." A loud moo interrupted Kiran. "They want to know which one you've chosen."

"If you're willing to help me prepare them and attend the show in Dunedin, I'll take both."

Gavin grinned. "Rohan might have some complaints, but it's fine with me. Kiran?"

Kiran hesitated, unsure of what Saber wanted from him. What Gavin expected as his boss. He might say it was fine, but that didn't mean there wouldn't be repercussions at a later date.

"Why don't you think about it?" Saber said. "Discuss it with Rohan and Ambar because I know you help out at the store as well. You can let me know in a couple of days. Could you tell the cattle they're both going to the show? And if you could tell them we're going to practice leading tomorrow morning when it's cooler, I'd appreciate it." He strode to the gate and opened it. "Ask them to return to the same paddock they were in this morning. I'll be there to open the gate shortly. Man, I wonder if I can clone you," he said, shaking his head. "I'll be back in ten."

"I told you Saber would be fine," Gavin said, clapping him over the back.

"Do you mind me working with him?"

"It's okay with me. You'll have to work with the cattle in the early morning or evenings anyway because of the heat. It won't affect work much."

"Thanks." The back of Kiran's neck started to itch again. "Gavin, can you take a look at the back of my neck? It's itchy as hell. It's become worse since I started to shift."

"Bend your head." Gavin walked behind him, and Kiran felt the pad of his finger smooth over the itchy spot. "It's inflamed."

"I've been scratching it a lot."

Gavin ran his finger over it, pressing harder.

Kiran flinched.

"I think there's something in there. Let me get my bag."

Saber arrived back after only five minutes. "Shifting the cows and calves normally takes ages. They walked straight to the gate and waited for me. One of the cows I picked licked me." He sounded bemused, and Kiran didn't think anything threw Saber. "What's up?"

"Come and look at the back of Kiran's neck," Gavin said.

"What is it?"

"Not sure." Gavin prodded with his finger again. "Kiran, I think I'll be able to dig whatever it is out, but it might hurt."

"Go ahead. The itching has been driving me crazy today."

Gavin pulled something silver from his bag and stepped behind Kiran, out of sight. Not being able to see the two men made Kiran nervous even though he knew they wouldn't hurt him. Something else he didn't understand about his character, although if the dreams were based on fact that might account for his distrust.

He felt a sharp burn.

"Don't move, Kiran." Gavin's tone held command, and he obeyed the order to remain still instantly.

"Is that what I think it is?" Saber asked.

"Yep, looks like a tracking device to me."

"A tracking device? Someone put a tracking device in me?" Hell, he didn't like the implications nor the fact someone felt they owned him or that they wanted to keep tabs on him.

"What do you want me to do with it?" Gavin asked Saber. "Should we destroy it? Don't move yet, Kiran. I want to put some antiseptic on the wound and a plaster. It's not bleeding much and you'll heal fast."

"I don't like this," Saber said, moving into Kiran's range of vision. "But if someone tracks you it might help you regain your memory."

"Someone tried to send me to the Auckland Zoo," Kiran snapped. "It's a safe bet I was meant for incarceration and someone wanted to dispose of me. It was bad enough before, knowing I might bring danger to Rohan and Ambar. But that tracking device is like a ticking bomb. My presence puts you all in danger."

Saber waited, listening. "We're a close-knit community. We protect what's ours, and you belong to us now."

Kiran's mouth opened and closed, not a sound emerging. *He belonged to them.* His throat tightened and he teared up. In his dreams, the chains had been real. He hadn't been a willing participant. This was different. The chains were imaginary, and he felt them as strongly as if they were real. Acceptance. He hadn't realized how much he'd craved it until this moment.

"We could leave the tracking device with Charlie and Laura at the police station. They could lock it up in evidence," Gavin said.

Saber nodded. "Yeah, I like that idea. We don't know if anyone will try to track you, but if they do, they'll have to enter the police station, and we'll have a warning of their presence. I'll take it down later and have a chat with Laura and Charlie."

"If someone went to the trouble of putting it in me, don't you think they'll want me back?" Kiran couldn't hide the touch of bitterness, the fear of the unknown. A thought occurred. "What if the zoo put it there?"

Gavin shook his head. "I worked with the Wellington Zoo for a few months when I was training. They use identification chips. They don't look anything like this."

Kiran turned to Saber. "Are you sure about this? I can leave Middlemarch and go somewhere else."

"I'm pretty sure Gavin doesn't want that. I don't. Rohan and Ambar might be a tad upset too," Saber said. "We'd like the three of you to stay. I'll put the word out and make sure everyone knows to watch for strangers. If someone comes looking they'll ask questions, which will make them stand out. Besides, we don't know the range of the tracking device. We might be making problems when there's no danger."

"You don't want to lose your animal whisperer," Gavin teased.

Saber raised his brows, looking every inch the leader. "And you want to lose the best assistant you could ever have?" His tone did nothing to quell Gavin's laughter. "No respect." Saber scowled. "You're as bad as my brothers."

"We like to keep you grounded," Gavin said. "Have you thought of introducing the twins to Ambar?"

"Hell, yeah, I thought about it, then developed a conscience," Saber said with feeling. "They do everything together. It's like double trouble, and I'd feel guilty inflicting them on someone I know. Emily says the twins will settle when they're ready, and they'll find someone. She stands up for them and thinks I don't notice her subtle attempts at matchmaking." Despite his disgruntled tone, Kiran heard the affection in his voice for both his wife and his brothers.

Kiran took a deep breath and said exactly what he felt. "I like Middlemarch, but putting everyone in danger worries me."

Saber patted him on the shoulder. "Together we're strong. That's what Emily says and she's right. Stay."

"Thank you. What will you tell everyone?"

"We'll tell the truth, but keep the animal whispering quiet. That's something we might be able to use at a later date. Don't worry," Saber said. "We'll cope with any problems."

Kiran nodded, thankful for the acceptance. Although he'd offered to leave, he had few resources. The rest of the day passed, Kiran feeling as if he lived in a horrid dream. He walked into the store, his problems a weighty burden.

"What's wrong?" Ambar glanced up from the magazine she was reading. "Never mind. You can tell me later. Rohan went home to start dinner." Ambar paused to glance at the clock behind her. "I'll be there in about forty minutes."

"Thanks." Kiran slipped behind the counter and gave her a brief hug. "Call us if you need help. We'll be here in minutes."

"Don't distract Rohan from dinner. I'm starving."

Kiran squeezed Ambar again before releasing her. "I can't promise that. I like distracting your brother."

Ambar's stern face softened. "I know. Get out of here."

Kiran smiled and left the store, heading for home. *Home.* Middlemarch, Rohan, and Ambar were his home now. Determination speared through him. Saber was right. He needed to stay. He needed to fight for what he wanted—love and Rohan.

Rohan was in the kitchen when he arrived, strains of a rock ballad pumping through the house.

"I miss Indian music," Kiran said, rounding the table and grabbing a seat at the breakfast bar so he could talk with Rohan. The scent of roast meat filled the kitchen along with chopped herbs.

Rohan grinned. "Yeah? Ambar and I don't. Our parents wouldn't let us listen to anything except Indian music while they were alive. We had to visit our friends to hear the music everyone else listened to. You remember Indian music?"

"Ah...hell if I know. It seemed like I did and now that you've asked me, I can't recall."

Rohan stirred a pot and replaced the lid. He turned it off and checked his watch. "We have time for a nap before Ambar gets home."

"I stopped at the store first. Ambar told me not to distract you."

"Ah, but I planned ahead. I made sure I cooked something that won't spoil. Besides, the oven timer is on."

"Something happened today."

"Tell me later. I need you now." He strode over to Kiran and placed Kiran's hand on his cock. It grew noticeably at his touch. "And not only do I need you, but I want you too." He grasped Kiran's hand. "Get naked and tell me about your day. It will make us both feel better."

Kiran let Rohan lead him from the kitchen and down the passage to their bedroom. Rohan seemed to sense his mood and undressed him slowly, kissing Kiran's bared skin as he removed one item of apparel at a time. As always, pleasure started to hum through his body. Rohan pushed him onto the bed and straddled his legs.

"I thought we were both getting naked."

"I thought so too," Rohan said. "I'm veering off course. Got distracted by the sight of your dick." He leaned over and gave the flared head a delicate lick. "Mmm, tastes good." Rohan took Kiran's cock into his mouth and went straight for the kill. He swirled his tongue across the head, over the underside, and applied hard suction. Sensation roared through Kiran. His hands curled into the navy blue and white quilt cover, creasing the cotton fabric while he bit back his cries of pleasure.

Rohan stopped what he was doing and lifted his head. "I know exactly what I'm doing. Don't even think about trying to hold back or remain silent. I want you to show me your pleasure. If something feels good, I want you to show appreciation. It makes me hot, Kiran. I love knowing I can make you feel good. I need it. Okay?" Rohan's intense expression told Kiran his open reactions were important.

"Okay. Rohan? You know I like anything you do to me." He frowned, suddenly angry with himself for not giving his lover the truth. He loved Rohan's touch, and he was pretty close to admitting his love for the man—at least to himself.

"I know." Rohan's voice held smugness. "I've felt how you tremble every time I touch you. Do you think I don't know you're trying to hold back because you're worried about your past? I understand. All I want is honesty. Don't shut me out. I wanted you from the moment I first saw you and love came pretty quickly after that." He smiled, his eyes glowing. "Yeah, it's true. I love you. You're my mate."

"Thank you." A weak response, but that was all he had, all he dared.

"Hell, don't thank me. We're a team. Together we're stronger. Mates." With a soft smile, he kissed Kiran's shaft. He fondled Kiran's balls, rolling them and took Kiran's cock back into his mouth, seemingly unworried by Kiran's failure to reciprocate by verbally admitting his love.

This time Kiran let the guilt slide away. He savored the sensations Rohan's hands and mouth plucked from his body. He shuddered and cried out, feeling the sharp release from his balls rushing up his cock and exploding into Rohan's mouth. He came down from the high slowly, realizing the sound of his loud breathing filled the bedroom. He became aware of the faint tick of Rohan's watch, the settling creak of the wood in the house. His eyes opened and he saw the dance of late afternoon sun through the blinds, Rohan's smile and the devilment in his eyes when he licked his lips.

Rohan stood, the mattress shifting under his release of weight. He stripped off rapidly before dropping beside Kiran. Their arms came around each other. They kissed, a slow meeting of lips and the giving of silent promises.

A team.

They smiled at each other when their lips parted.

"What happened today that has you so rattled?" Rohan asked.

"Gavin dug a tracking device out of the back of my neck."

Rohan stilled, his eyes narrowing. "No shit?"

"I'm thinking we could all be in a lot of trouble if the tracking device is working properly."

Rohan nodded, looking serious for once. "What happened?"

"We were with Saber. They've decided to put the tracking device at the police station and everyone will watch for strangers who act weird."

A splutter escaped Rohan. "Ambar's convinced some of the local farmers are weird. The single ones, anyway, because they're haunting the store. Are you sure strangers would stand out?"

"You know what I mean."

Rohan sobered. "Sorry. There's no need to feel guilty. You didn't know the tracking device was there. This isn't your fault. You didn't exactly volunteer to go to the zoo."

"But you don't know about my dreams, the kinky stuff I've been dreaming."

"The dreams don't mean a thing. Don't let them define you." Rohan's voice softened. "I'm not the only one who cares about you. Ambar likes you. You've made friends, and we want to help. Don't shut us out or think you must leave. Let us help you. Let us show our love and friendship."

Rohan's words made him feel weak and strong at the same time. "I'll try."

"Good." Rohan checked his watch again and smiled. "We have time to get off and shower before Ambar gets home."

Rohan's husky tone had Kiran's cock reacting in a flash. "What did you have in mind?"

Rohan crawled closer and thrust his hips. His erection slid across Kiran's hipbone and came to a rest against Kiran's cock. "How about some rubbing action? Or whatever makes us feel good."

"I like the way you think." Kiran's eyes closed and he blindly sought Rohan's mouth, sighing with pleasure when their tongues swirled together. Their hips moved, shafts rubbing together with each lazy rock.

Kiran surrendered to the sensual banquet, his last sensible thought that Saber and Rohan were right. Running wouldn't solve a thing. Middlemarch was part of him now and he didn't want to leave.

CHAPTER EIGHT

THREE WEEKS LATER

A TOUCH OF PANIC filled Nando as he picked up the rental car on his second visit to Auckland. He had to locate Kiran this time. It was obvious the man was in hiding. Nando knew the slave couldn't leave the country because he didn't possess travel documents. Someone must be helping him because he'd entered the country as a tiger, after Nando's fool employees had sold Kiran to make some quick rupees. They'd been smart enough to provide counterfeit papers for the tiger, which meant Kiran had ended up at a zoo. Nando had traveled around the Auckland area and gone north, trying to pick up the tracking device David had planted in Kiran when he'd first arrived at the family home. Great foresight on his brother's part. Great foresight on his part when he'd copied his brother's files, hoping to find information he could use to his benefit.

This visit he'd managed to score a visa for three months. He'd search south until he picked up a signal.

Kiran couldn't live.

The possibility of the slave's return to India put Nando's entire future in jeopardy. No, Kiran would die as would anyone who got in his way. Nando thought about calling for help and rejected it. That would require telling others the truth, giving explanations. He had to handle this himself.

Nando programmed the directional system in the car and pulled out of the car park to head south. He'd figured he'd drive down the middle of the North Island, and if he didn't have any luck, he'd catch the ferry across Cook Strait and start searching in the south. If he hit Queenstown before he found Kiran, he figured he'd do a bungee jump after all because he'd sure as hell need something to channel his stress by that stage.

No, he'd find Kiran before he reached the bottom of the South Island. From his observations of Kiran's relationship with his oldest brother, he knew Kiran had a subservient nature. It wouldn't be difficult to slip into David's role, although he wasn't interested in fucking the man.

He'd use Kiran's obedience against him and kill him. Simple. Mess sorted. He could continue with his life.

Nando checked the road sign, took the motorway turnoff and headed south with the silent tracking beacon mocking him.

"Where is Nando?" At the back of David's mind, he registered his calm and cool tone. It surprised him since his mind boiled with anger. Fury held his muscles rigid, and he didn't think he'd manage to release the emotion until he learned the truth.

The full truth.

So far he'd learned his younger brothers were lazy and weak. Nando had taken over the business decisions for the family assets under their direction. Their youngest brother had both intelligence and innate slyness that hadn't been obvious to David until he'd scratched beneath the surface. He studied the three men who stood before him. They were vain and weak.

"He said he had business matters to take care of," Jay said.

"Where?" David demanded.

"I don't know. I didn't ask." Isa pouted. "He does a good job."

"He brought lowlifes into this house. He entertained them with my slaves." And he'd lost Kiran because of it. He'd thought his slave was safe. A hard ache struck in the region of his heart, and he struggled for composure, his nails digging into his palms as he imagined throttling his brothers. "Now I find that not all the slaves were killed by the so-called fake virus."

David turned to his next brother. "Where is Nando?"

"I am ashamed, my brother. I do not know," Suman said.

David turned away in disgust. "This will change. You will pull your weight and carry out your assigned duties or you will leave." He wasn't sure where to turn next since he didn't know any of Nando's contacts. His mouth firmed with resolution. He might not know now, but he would continue until he learned of Kiran's fate. Until he knew for sure his slave—the man he loved—was dead, he refused to give up his search.

"Nando was having an affair with the prime minister's daughter," Isa said. "Perhaps she knows his location."

"Thank you," David said, his mind sprinting ahead to consider how he might approach the woman. "I have rearranged my schedule. My secretary has duties for you all. If you don't wish to work for the family business tell her and vacate the premises before I return."

David walked away, amusement at their muttered grumbles about his Hitler secretary finding substance in a stark smile. He didn't have time to baby them. It was obvious he'd allowed their father's wishes to get the better of his good sense. It wouldn't happen again. David didn't make mistakes twice.

Kiran, I'm so sorry. I'm coming, my love. We will be together again soon, in this life or the next.

"You look nice, Ambar," Kiran said, taking note of her short black skirt and the length of slender, toned leg on display. Her red and white top was close-fitting but tasteful, and she had an excited glow in her cheeks as she entered the kitchen. He could feel Rohan's brain ticking and wondered if Rohan had come to the same conclusion he had. A date.

He and Rohan were having a beer before dinner. The scent of basil, tomatoes and meat filled the room since they'd decided to eat pasta for dinner. His cooking was improving, and he took pleasure in the new skill, although he was still nowhere near Rohan and Ambar's level of competence.

Rohan took his hand off Kiran's knee and scowled at his sister. "Why aren't you eating here tonight?"

"I'm going on a date," Ambar announced as she joined them at the dinner table.

Bingo! Kiran glanced at Rohan and as one they turned their attention to Ambar.

"Who with?" Rohan asked as he kicked off his sandals.

"Where are you going?" Kiran asked, setting his beer on the table.

"I'm only going to answer because I know you both care about me. Neither of you have the right to veto my date. I'm going out with Jake Quinn, and we're driving to Mosgiel for dinner."

"That's a long drive," Rohan said.

Ambar shrugged, but Kiran sensed the combination of tension and excitement inside her. "Would you rather I went to Jake's place and had dinner?" she added, her chin lifting in defiance.

"No!" Kiran said, thinking of all the ways she could get in trouble at Jake's place. His eyes narrowed and he took a deep breath. It eased out while he waited for Rohan to react.

"Jeez, guys. Rohan, why couldn't you have been straight? Then I would have had another woman to back me up." She wrinkled her nose at Kiran. "Right now I feel like I have two big brothers."

"Good," Rohan said.

"Yeah, you make sure Jake knows you have two brothers," Kiran said. "That way he'll be less inclined to take liberties."

"Jake is human. I think I can take care of one male human."

"You shouldn't act overconfident. He could drug your food or drink," Kiran said. "You'd be helpless then."

"Is that what happened to you?" Ambar shot back.

"I..." Kiran trailed off, his brow furrowing in concentration. In the dim recesses of his mind a memory teased him before slipping away. "I don't know," he said in frustration.

Ambar reached over and squeezed his shoulder. "I'm sorry."

"No," Rohan said with a sigh. "We're sorry for questioning you. We care about you. Can you at least ring us when you're on the way home?"

"And can we meet Jake?" Kiran asked. "We promise to be on our best behavior."

Ambar visibly hesitated. "He's been in the store."

A knock on the door interrupted their argument, and Rohan leapt to his feet. "I'll get it."

"Rohan—"

Kiran halted her with a smile. "We promise not to interrogate him or scare him off. Please."

Ambar gave a clipped nod and relaxed a fraction. Rohan sent him a grateful smile and turned away to answer the door. Rohan's smile warmed him inside.

"Thanks for going out for the night, Ambar. I appreciate the way you try to give us privacy."

Ambar grinned. "Are you kidding? You make Rohan happy. I love seeing him like this, although tonight is for me too. Jake isn't like the other guys who come into the store. He doesn't look at me as if he's imagining me naked."

"All guys do that, Ambar," Kiran said.

"*Eew.*"

"Not me. I only imagine Rohan naked."

"I'm pleased to hear it," Rohan said.

"Oh heck," Ambar said, and Kiran wanted to laugh out loud at the burst of color on her cheeks. "You guys promised not to embarrass me."

Kiran stood and offered his hand to the tall brown-haired man at Rohan's side. "I'm Kiran."

"Jake Quinn," he said, not hesitating to take Kiran's hand. "I'm pleased to meet you. I think I've seen you with Gavin Finlay out at my father's farm. He said you're both good with the stock, which is high praise from him."

"Thanks," Kiran said.

"Have fun on your date," Rohan said.

Ambar rolled her eyes. "You're not gonna wait up for me."

"Of course not," Kiran said, unable to resist teasing her. "Rohan and I are gonna make some noise. We have to hold back a little when you're here."

"The two of you are impossible," Ambar muttered. "Come on, Jake. Let's go. There's no telling what they're going to say next."

"Nice to meet you both," Jake said, seemingly unperturbed by their relationship.

"Likewise," Rohan said. "Maybe Ambar will let us talk with you next time."

"Impossible," Ambar said, but she paused to kiss her brother and repeated the kiss with Kiran.

Kiran was only vaguely aware of them leaving. He lifted his hand and brushed his fingers over the spot Ambar had kissed. Family. He'd found a real family. He didn't know why but the fact kept astonishing him, and he liked to reinforce the thought in his own mind.

"What's wrong?" Rohan asked. "Did you sense something wrong about Jake?"

"No. No, I think Ambar can take care of herself. He seems fine. She kissed me."

Rohan frowned. "Should I be worried about that?"

"No, I mean she likes me."

"What's not to like?"

Kiran rubbed his hands over his face. "Hell, I'm not explaining this well. Ambar made me feel like a member of the family."

Rohan's scowl smoothed out. "Because she thinks of you as another brother. You've got the teasing thing down, and she knows how I feel about you. Why shouldn't she treat you as family?"

"It feels weird in a good way. I don't think I've had a family before."

Rohan tugged him into his arms and cupped his face with his hands. "You have one now, along with a lot of friends. Do you feel like eating?"

"Not really."

"Good." Rohan stepped back and captured Kiran's hand. "Wanna fool around?"

Kiran's pulse quickened with anticipation, his instinctive response powerful and physical. All the blood in his body rushed to his groin. He grinned at his lover, savoring the rush of pleasure, of eagerness. "Always."

Rohan switched off the elements on the stove. "I'm tempted to fool around in the kitchen, but Ambar would kill us if she found out."

Kiran chuckled, picturing the scene and let Rohan lead him down the passage to the room they shared. Rohan closed the door after them, enclosing them in their private haven.

During the weeks since they'd started to share a bedroom, they'd unpacked properly and the room had taken on their personalities. It was restful in shades of blue, the wooden surfaces shiny and dust free. Kiran had discovered he liked to draw and they'd pinned his sketches of animals and people he met on a corkboard. Rohan wanted him to draw a mural on one wall, but they hadn't decided on the subject matter yet.

"Strip," Rohan said.

Immediately, Kiran whipped his T-shirt over his head and tossed it aside. He toed off his shoes and yanked off the rest of his clothes. He stilled when he realized Rohan stared at him. "What?"

"I love you. I want to mark you, take you as my mate."

Kiran sank to the bed, his knees buckling at the expression of stark desire on Rohan's face. "But I still don't know about my past. How can you want me? Once the mark is bestowed it's final and can't be undone, right? What if my memory returns and I'm not the person—"

"Stop right there. You don't have a mark now, which means you're free. If you had a mate, the mark would still be there unless your mate had died. You're a good man, Kiran. You're the man I want. I'd like everyone to know it."

"Can I think about it?" The idea that Rohan wanted to stake such a final claim blew him away. A quick scan of Rohan's face told Kiran that Rohan meant exactly what he said.

"Yeah."

"Are you pissed?"

Rohan scowled. "A little. You worry about the past too much. I keep telling you it's the future that matters. I thought you were okay with that."

Kiran stood and took three giant steps to reach Rohan. "I want you so much."

Their lips met, the kiss hard and full of ownership. Kiran let his worries fade under the sensual onslaught, responding to Rohan with every particle in his body. He slipped his hands beneath the hem of Rohan's polo shirt and slid his palms over the warm skin of his back and broad shoulders.

Rohan sucked on his tongue, the sensation shooting straight to his groin. Kiran moaned and pressed closer, pumping his hips against Rohan to get some friction going on his cock.

"Someone's impatient," Rohan said.

"And someone isn't naked. As much as I like the way you fill out those jeans, I'd like to see you strip."

"Why don't you do it for me?" The lazy suggestion held a silent dare, one Kiran was happy to meet.

Instead of undressing Rohan immediately, Kiran started to tease him, dipping one hand into the back of his jeans and running the fingers of the other up and down his fly. He explored. He tempted. He used every method he knew to make Rohan hot and desperate.

Kiran shuffled Rohan over to the bed and they fell in a tangle of limbs with Rohan on top. Rohan grinned at him, another hint of challenge.

"I'm on top. What ya gonna do?"

"Deal with it," Kiran said, drawing his head down. His kiss was aggressive this time, noses clashing until they lined up right. Rohan's taste went through him, a hint of hops from the beer they'd shared before their aborted dinner and the unique smoky flavor he'd come to associate with his lover. He nipped and smoothed away the sting with a lick of his tongue. Every part of his body tightened and prepared for the loving to come. Rohan made him feel free, made him feel whole. Special. Loved.

Kiran hesitated at the thought, tried it for size and knew it was true. He truly believed Rohan loved him and wouldn't intentionally hurt him.

"Okay, I agree." Kiran stared up into Rohan's eyes. "Mark me."

Rohan pushed away with a sound of disgust. "Don't do me any favors."

Not the reaction he'd hoped for, but he didn't blame Rohan. He'd hesitated, his past looming large in his mind yet again. Kiran grabbed Rohan before he could lever off the bed. "You're right to doubt my decision considering the way I've hesitated. It's hard sometimes. When I try to look back, all I see is this black abyss. It scares me—the not knowing. The dreams."

The stiffness leached from Rohan's muscles, and Kiran relaxed his grip. "I know what I feel. I'm not about to change my mind."

"Neither am I," Kiran said with a soft smile. "I've never felt like this before. Not in my memory." Although he wanted to say words of love, he faltered.

Rohan curved his body against Kiran's in silent acceptance, and Kiran released the breath he hadn't been aware of holding.

"Tell me about the marking process again," he said.

Rohan frowned and scanned Kiran's face. Whatever he saw must have reassured him because he rolled off Kiran to lie on his back and started talking.

"It's the way feline's mate. According to Saber, most felines sense their mate when they meet them. There's an overriding urge to grab them and never let go. Sex jumps to the fore and it's hard to imagine ever having sex with anyone else. You want to touch, to fuck and then do it all over again." Rohan stroked his hand over Kiran's jaw, the subtle pressure of his fingers making Kiran turn to face him. They stared at each other, and Kiran fancied he could

187

see Rohan's heart in his eyes. "Remember how you felt when Ambar and I rescued you from the hospital. You didn't know me but you wanted to have sex. That's the mating urge."

"Can you feel that urge and walk away?"

"Yeah, nothing is final until the marking process is complete, but the craving is hard to fight. That's where a feline bites his mate on the shoulder. Here," he said, touching his fingers to the fleshy part where Kiran's neck and shoulder met. "This is the marking spot. The bite draws blood and enzymes enter the blood. The wound heals to a small scar."

"And if both lovers are feline?"

"They can exchange bites, usually while making love. Or not exchange bites. It depends on the relationship." Rohan's gaze skittered away from him and tension filled the room.

Kiran frowned. "But wouldn't that mean the unmarked person could walk away?"

"Yes, if they wanted to." Rohan darted a quick look at him then lowered his gaze. The truth seared Kiran. Rohan feared that happening to him but had still suggested the marking to Kiran. The knowledge humbled Kiran, filled him with both wonder and hope.

"And what happens if one of the partners dies?" Kiran asked.

"They mourn their lost partner, but eventually the mark fades. They can mate again if they find someone they care for."

"But if they mark each other, they stay together for life? They can't stray or leave for another?"

"No, there's something about the marking process that makes you stay true to your partner. It's impossible for marked partners to cheat on each other."

"And the instinct to mark is never wrong or false?"

"Never. Meeting a true mate is a process of fate or kismet. I've known many couples who have married and lived together but haven't mated and have never found anyone to tempt them. My parents had an arranged marriage. Many tiger shifters have arranged marriages and are perfectly happy without going through the marking process."

"Meeting you and Ambar was kismet. It saved my life." At the time, Kiran hadn't realized the danger they'd faced to save him. He knew it now. He also sensed he'd never felt as happy or fulfilled as he did now. "I don't have any doubts, Rohan. When I think about my future, I can't imagine one without you. Mark me and I'll mark you in return."

Rohan turned to face him then, and Kiran saw the sparkle of unshed tears in his eyes. "Thank you."

"Stand up. Let me undress you."

Rohan pushed off the bed and Kiran followed him. Kiran kissed him, a slow, lingering touch and taste of lips. He nipped Rohan's bottom lip, laughing when his lover jerked away with a curse.

"Let me kiss it better," he whispered, peeling the cotton fabric over Rohan's shoulders. Once he freed the polo shirt from Rohan's arms and over his head, he tossed it away. He breathed in the citrus tang of Rohan's soap and nibbled on his jaw. Rohan tilted his head and Kiran kissed over his jaw and down his neck, savoring the contrast of stubble and warm skin. When he reached the marking site, Rohan shuddered. Kiran felt the race of Rohan's heart, and his own heart rate kicked up into a similar speedy beat. The instinct to bite roared through him. It was as if his mind had finally synchronized with his body, the urge seductive. Unbearable. With steely control, he licked, keeping his teeth covered by his lips even though every sense roared at him to take action and his gums burned as his canines pushed to the surface.

"Hell," Rohan said, his voice unsteady and filled with longing. "Can you take my jeans off for me? And watch your claws. They're bloody sharp."

Kiran looked at his hands with surprise. Beneath the nails of his human fingers, lines of black were clearly visible, the sharp ends protruding and digging into Rohan's shoulders. "I've started to change," he said in amazement. As he recognized the shift in his body, his canines forced down fully from his gums.

"Side effect of the mating process," Rohan said, his voice distorted. Kiran caught the flash of canines when Rohan spoke.

"Interesting." It seemed his body was already with the program.

"Jeans," Rohan reminded him. "They're strangling me." He gave a lopsided grin. "Could cause some damage if you don't hurry."

"That right?" Kiran rose from the bed and tugged Rohan with him.

"You're not suffering because I liberated you."

Silence fell as their eyes met. "So you did, and I'm glad it was you." Kiran unfastened Rohan's jeans, carefully maneuvering the coarse fabric over his hard-on. He pushed the denim and underwear down his legs and helped him step out of them. Kiran straightened and wrapped his arms around Rohan, holding him despite the urgency beating through his body.

Taking Kiran's hand, Rohan led him back to the bed.

"Face-to-face," Rohan said. "I want to watch your face when you mark me."

Kiran's eyes narrowed as he dropped to the bed. "I thought you'd go first. What if I do it wrong?" Then it hit him. Rohan still wasn't convinced he meant to go through with the marking. He held doubts regarding Kiran's commitment. He nodded. "I'll go first. Tell me exactly what to do."

"Bite me here," Rohan said, fingering the spot he'd indicated earlier. "Bite down until you taste blood and hold me tight. I'm not sure of exactly what happens because I haven't seen it done." His words emerged with a faint lisp.

"You want me to bite you now?"

Rohan chuckled and snuggled up to his side. "Wait until I'm inside you. The bite hurts and the pleasure of sex helps with the pain."

"Fuck, I don't want to harm you."

"You won't." Confidence filled Rohan's voice and it calmed Kiran's jittery nerves. Excitement pulsed through him instead, and his feline pushed beneath his skin. A low growl rumbled through his mind. "It feels as if my feline is pacing the length of my body. I feel as if I might jump out of my skin."

"Tell me about it." Rohan bared his teeth. The canines extended fully from his upper jaw, which accounted for the lisp in his speech.

They kissed again, hands getting busy as they touched and stroked each other, mindful of the claws they both sported. Every touch seemed special, more than sex. Much more. Kiran trembled with the urgency thrumming through the air. Rohan kissed his hip and turned his head, nuzzling his cheek against Kiran's cock.

"Suck me," Kiran said, wanting to feel Rohan's mouth more than anything.

"I might hurt you with my teeth. I can't seem to make them disappear." A wry smile accompanied the statement. "That's what you do to me."

Kiran hesitated when he saw the sharp teeth. "You won't hurt me." He hoped. He snorted. He was about to hurt Rohan. A little pain in exchange wasn't so bad. Funnily enough, he wasn't worried about the mark Rohan would bestow on him.

Rohan's tongue flicked out, rasping across the tender skin of his tip. He lapped up the drops of pre-cum, making a humming sound of appreciation as he did so.

Unable to help himself, Kiran bucked against the rasp of Rohan's tongue, pressing against Rohan's lips. Instead of following his plea, Rohan grasped his shaft and pumped it hard, his grip firm and almost painful. He continued with the punishing grip and dipped his head to lick Kiran's sac. His balls were firm and hard, drawn up tight with arousal. He paused to grab a pillow and shoved it under Kiran's hips before continuing with the torture. Damn, Kiran loved the way Rohan touched him. A finger skimmed his hole, delicately firing nerve endings. Then the warm rasp of a tongue continued, and Kiran groaned, his excitement building.

Tongue and finger tempted him, teased him, drove him crazy. Rohan took his time, preparing him even though he didn't need much. Every touch and careful stroke burned into his memory, and he knew he'd never forget this day. *Never.*

Rohan added lube to the equation and pressed inside Kiran.

"Have I ever told you how good you feel?" Rohan asked. "The tight clamp of your arse, the heat. It's amazing. I want to have you in me when I mark you."

Kiran gasped. He'd thought about fucking Rohan, but had only thought it because he was happy to receive, but the idea grabbed hold now, the moment Rohan uttered it. "I'd like that."

"Haven't done it for a long time," Rohan confessed. "It won't matter. We'll manage."

Rohan started to move. Steady strokes designed to push both of them into pleasure. Kiran's eyes fluttered closed, and Rohan halted, fully embedded in him.

"Open your sexy eyes, Kiran. I want to see you properly. Yeah. Just like that."

The pleasure ramped up inside Kiran, his breathing coming in harsh gasps. He nuzzled Rohan's neck and realized instinct guided him. His tongue rasped across the fleshy part, and he heard Rohan's moan of pleasure, felt the tremor of his body. His teeth gazed the site and Rohan's thrusts became choppy. A stroke hit his gland and he bit down, pleasure firing through his balls. Then he came and the metallic taste of Rohan's blood filled his mouth. Instinctively, he licked and the bleeding seemed to slow. Rohan moaned, his cock pulsing deep in Kiran's ass. He jerked and moaned again. Kiran couldn't tell if pain lashed him or pleasure. Hell, what if he'd injured him? His teeth still gripped Rohan's shoulder.

Kiran released the grip of his teeth, licked again and lifted his head. He studied the angry mark and saw minimal bleeding. "Are you okay?"

"Shit that hurt." Rohan's bright eyes held awe, as if he'd never expected anything like that.

"Is it still sore? It's not bleeding but I've made a mess. It looks like a bite." Now he was worried. "Maybe I should call Gavin."

"I don't think I've ever felt so much pleasure at the same time. That was amazing. You're amazing, Kiran."

Relief seeped into him. "So you're okay?"

"Very okay. It's like an extra sense has kicked in. Can you feel it?"

Kiran listened with his senses and blinked when he experienced a connection with Rohan. He'd been so scared he'd hurt Rohan, he hadn't listened to the shimmer of knowledge zipping through his mind. "That's amazing. I can't read your thoughts or anything but it's like an awareness, an extra sense."

Rohan separated their bodies and stood to head for the bathroom.

Kiran heard the rush of water as Rohan cleaned up. He should move but he hadn't felt so relaxed in ages. He luxuriated in it, letting his eyes slide shut even though his mind moved rapidly, recalling the moment when he'd clamped down on Rohan's shoulder, the way his world had shifted into rightness.

Rohan entered the bedroom. "Lift up."

Kiran opened his eyes and saw Rohan had a cloth, and he smiled as the other man tended him. "That was amazing."

"Good," Rohan said and returned the cloth to the bathroom. He strode back across the room to the bed, a naked man comfortable in his skin. "Because we're gonna fool around some more then I'm going to mark you."

"Tonight?"

Rohan stilled, his fingers creeping up to touch his mark. It didn't hurt exactly, not like he thought it would. Instead the brush of his fingers sent a roar of delight directly to his cock. Shaking his thoughts back to Kiran, he said, "You have a problem with that?"

"No problem. I don't think we'll have to fool around much." Kiran indicated his erection with a self-deprecating grin.

Rohan pulled his fingers away from the mark and it hit him. He'd pushed the idea of marking because he was frightened Kiran would gain his memory and leave him. Yeah, Kiran could still leave, but it would take more effort. A sliver of guilt pierced him then. Had he forced Kiran into the mating? While he was sure of what he wanted, had he pressured Kiran? It must be difficult not knowing about the past. He hesitated, swallowed and honor forced him to speak.

"Kiran, do you want me to mark you? I mean are you sure?"

Kiran's dark brows rose. "Isn't it too late for second thoughts now? I've marked you."

"No, it's not too late. I want to make sure I haven't pressured you into the marking."

"And if I said no?" Kiran watched him closely, the atmosphere in the bedroom suddenly strained.

Disappointment and pain slapped Rohan. He had to fight to keep the hurt from his face. "If you don't want me to mark you in return tonight, I won't force the issue. I'm sure of my feelings. I've never felt like this about any other man. I want to spend the rest of my days with you, but I want your happiness more. We can do this another time." It almost killed him to say the words, to force them past the growing lump in his throat.

"You would do that for me?" Kiran asked. "Put me first even though that's not what you want?"

Yeah, he'd do it for Kiran, even if it killed him "Yes."

Kiran's mouth stretched into a curve, the brilliant smile echoed in his eyes. He held out his hand to Rohan. "You're a man any feline would proudly call mate. We're finishing this marking thing now because it's what I want. Really. I've never been so sure of anything in my life."

For an instant Rohan stared, dazzled by Kiran's handsome face and beautiful blue-green eyes, then his words registered. He wanted to complete the mating, tying them together. Joy washed over him, filling his heart and the empty place in his soul, one he hadn't realized he possessed. "Thank you," he said, his throat clogged with emotion. "Damn, I love you."

Kiran held out his hand. "Come here."

Rohan clasped Kiran's hands, savored the bite of his fingers as they gripped and drew him closer. Their gazes met, held. Silent messages passed between them, acceptance and understanding.

They kissed, hunger driving Rohan, making him want to stake a claim and be claimed. His urgency leapt to Kiran and soon their bodies strained against each other, chests rubbed and cocks ground together. Choppy breathing interspersed with whispers of love. Rohan rolled, taking Kiran with him.

Rohan grinned up at Kiran. "Your turn."

"What if I hurt you? This doesn't seem familiar to me at all."

"Sure, it might hurt, but it will be good at the same time. I'd like you to do this, but if you don't want to that's okay."

"What does it feel like?"

"It's amazing. It's like being part of you. You're tight and hot and I love the way you go crazy when I hit you in the right spot. What do you want to do?"

"Everything," Kiran said without hesitation. "I'm trying to forget the lack of past but sometimes it's easy to slip back into the black hole. It's hard not to worry."

Rohan nibbled Kiran's biceps and licked the letter K over the bulging muscle before he answered. "I know, but you're not alone. Remember that. You're a good man, Kiran. Don't let anyone try to tell you different." He paused. "Why don't you grab the lube?"

Kiran's eyes widened, his chest and shoulders jerked in a noticeable quake before he reached for the bottle Rohan had left sitting on the nightstand. He fingered the mark he'd put on Rohan and jerked away when Rohan gasped and arched against him. Their cocks slid together in a sensual kiss and they both groaned.

"Damn, if you do that again I don't think I'll last long. It felt as if you'd lit a fuse."

"Good to know," Kiran said, a hot gleam in his eyes. He moved down Rohan's body, pausing to stroke and kiss, taking more time than Rohan had ever seen him use before. It made Rohan realize that although Kiran participated with enthusiasm, he didn't initiate anything.

Rohan made a mental note to encourage Kiran to explore and lead, not that he minded taking the dominant role, but sometimes it felt damn good to receive attention from a lover. He hissed out a breath when Kiran's hot mouth closed over his cock and he started to suck. Like now. Not even the faint bite of a sharp canine pushing against the side of his cock detracted from his excitement. He grasped the pleasure and rode it, exhilarated by the sensual hum crawling through his body. He registered the faint hiss the lube bottle made when squeezed and his excitement intensified. Seconds later a slippery finger stroked across his hole. The suction of Kiran's mouth distracted him from the initial intrusion, but careful strokes across his gland grabbed his attention.

"Hell," he muttered, the automatic jolt of his hips pushing him deeper into Kiran's mouth.

The vibration around his cock told him Kiran was laughing while the pump of a finger in his ass told him Kiran was either a natural or he'd had previous experience. Another finger joined the first and the scissoring action opened him. Need roared out of control, a desperation to come.

"Damn, Kiran. You're killing me, man."

Kiran lifted his head, releasing his cock with a faint pop. "Good, I must be doing it right."

Rohan swallowed the demand for Kiran to suck his cock again. This was Kiran's show, and besides, Rohan didn't think Kiran's mouth should be anywhere near his delicate parts when Rohan marked his shoulder. The last thing they needed was an embarrassing emergency call to Gavin. They'd never hear the end of it despite medical confidentiality because Ambar would find out and tell everyone. He paused then he realized the contortions they'd have to go through for his thought to come true. He snorted. He was nervous and not thinking right.

"Rohan?"

"Any better and we'll have to call Gavin."

Kiran laughed. "Yeah, wouldn't that be a kick?" He removed his fingers, leaving Rohan feeling empty and still needy.

The bottle sounded its distinctive squelch again. Rohan's heart thudded three hard beats.

"You okay?"

"Eager," Rohan confessed. "Empty."

"I can fix that."

"They why are you talking so much? Fix it for me."

Kiran laughed, his bark of humor calming some of the impatience and angst in Rohan. Kiran moved and Rohan closed his eyes, the darkness highlighting every sensation bombarding his senses. The faint pressure against his entrance brought a rush of both anticipation and a sweet burn.

He wanted to tell Kiran to take it slow, to give him orders as to what to do and how to do it. He didn't, remaining silent and still, waiting to learn what Kiran would do next. Kiran withdrew a fraction and returned, pushing farther this time. He leaned over Rohan and kissed his neck using a combination of sucking and nibbles, the rasp of his tongue. Then Kiran placed his mouth over his mark and gently laved it with his tongue. Once again the surge of lust and pleasure took him by surprise. His entire body bucked, impaling Kiran's cock deeper.

Face-to-face, with Rohan's cock trapped between their bodies, they moved in an increasingly faster dance. Kiran withdrew and thrust in slow even strokes until his cock fully impaled him.

Kiran lifted his head and sought his lips. The kiss was sweet, almost chaste, but it said more than words ever could to Rohan. Kiran loved him. If he would only say the words...

Kiran's breathing became labored, his large body shuddering in Rohan's arms. Rohan wanted to ask if it was still okay for him to bite. He wanted permission but fear kept him quiet. There was still a tiny part of him that doubted Kiran. Shoving the anxiety away, he focused on the pleasure, the cock filling his ass, the scent of sex, of Kiran. The touch of Kiran's mouth. The friction as the head of his cock rubbed Kiran's chest.

"Rohan, I understand what you meant. This feels so good." Kiran punctuated his words with a leisurely stroke until he filled Rohan.

Rohan groaned, his balls so tight he thought they might burst. Each time with Kiran felt better than the last. He gripped Kiran's shoulders and nuzzled his neck. "Touch my mark again," he said. "Please." He turned the abrupt order into a plea.

Kiran covered Rohan's mark with his mouth and sucked lightly. The jolt of pleasure made Rohan moan out loud. Before the thought even registered, he bit down on the fleshy part of Kiran's neck, the roar of ecstasy making his toes curl. He tasted Kiran's blood as he came, the spurt of semen trapped between their clammy bodies. Kiran's warm breath caressed his mark, and he was vaguely aware of Kiran coming as well. They collapsed together in a heaving pile, both gasping for air.

"That was amazing," Kiran said in a low voice. "Intense. I don't think I've ever come so hard in all my life." He ran his fingers over Rohan's chin and placed a kiss on his jawbone, almost purring as he rubbed against Rohan.

Rohan took a look at his shoulder. "Shit, you're bleeding still." Rohan flicked his tongue over the wound, cleaning it gently.

"I...will it always feel so sensitive?" Kiran asked, shuddering. "Every time you touch it, my cock twitches." With another soft gasp, Kiran pulled away and stood. He stumbled from the bedroom, and Rohan heard running water.

Sighing, he placed his hands behind his head. Pleasure and well-being suffused his entire body. Kiran appeared with a cloth in hand and handed it to Rohan.

"Thanks. You okay?" Rohan's gaze went to the livid mark on Kiran's shoulder. At least it wasn't bleeding now. He took care of cleanup and waited in silence while Kiran returned the cloth to the bathroom. "Kiran?"

Kiran was difficult to read sometimes but he felt a connection, stronger now than before. He thought his new mate was okay but he wanted confirmation.

Kiran joined him on the bed, sliding his arms around Rohan. He pressed a kiss on Rohan's shoulder and smiled. "I feel great. Really great." *That was amazing.*

Rohan froze. Had he imagined that? Kiran's thoughts in his mind. In a test, he thought, *I love you. I'm so glad we found each other.*

Holy shit! Kiran stared at him. *I can hear your thoughts.*

I couldn't hear them until after I marked you. "Wow," Rohan whispered. "That's amazing."

They grinned at each other, and the residual tension inside Rohan seeped away. They were marked mates now, and they had the future in front of them. A future together.

CHAPTER NINE

Kiran slipped into sleep, cuddled in Rohan's arms. Almost immediately the dreams started.

Blood. *So much blood*.

It ran across the floor, soaking into his clothes, covering his body.

Horror shook his hand as he pushed to his knees and stood, the tiles cold beneath his bare feet. He blinked, took an involuntary step forward, almost slipping in the puddle.

A moan of terror escaped. Three bodies. Two women and one man. Naked. Their throats cut. Numerous cuts on the rest of their bodies. Horror in their wide, staring eyes.

His gaze zeroed in on the bloody knife. The blade gleamed dully from the floor, not far from where he stood.

Footsteps sounded in the passage outside the room. The doorknob rattled. He whirled to see the door open. At the back of his mind, he noted his bloody footprints as he backed away, his heart pounding in fear.

"Holy hell. What happened?" the man in the doorway asked. His voice was rough and smoky. Low and soothing, yet the hair at the back of Kiran's neck prickled in warning.

"I don't know." And he didn't. He had no memory of how he'd arrived in this room or what had happened. Kiran took another step, distancing himself from the man, pressing into the wall at his back. Fear was a tight band around his chest. His breath came in raspy gasps, tinged with panic, especially when the man smiled at him. That smile didn't reach his eyes, and Kiran knew he was in trouble. The man thought he'd committed this atrocity. Another thought occurred and he sensed the truth of this new one. The man knew who'd done this and intended to blame him.

The man scanned the room. He didn't enter, his expression didn't change. "Did you do this?"

"No!" Kiran's denial rang with truth and a touch of revulsion. How could the man think he'd murdered his friends? He would never hurt another living creature, let alone one of his friends. It didn't matter how much blood covered his clothes or how big the gap in his memory, he knew he hadn't done this to his friends.

"That's not what it looks like to me." The soothing tone turned accusing, and Kiran's dread grew proportionately. "Come with me."

"No. I didn't kill them."

The man didn't listen. He shouted for a guard, and two came running. They escorted Kiran to a room and shoved him inside, locking the door after him.

The tiny room was dark. Cold.

Kiran sank to the floor, his thin tunic and cotton trousers no barrier to the chill seeping through the floor and walls. He shivered, his thoughts as dark as the room. Time ticked away. His eyes adjusted to the gloom. Kiran wrapped his arms around his knees in an attempt to keep warm.

Helpless anger burned in him. They intended to blame him for the deaths. Damn, he was so cold. A rumbling growl sounded in his mind. Agitated and terrified, he pushed to his feet and started to pace. Back and forward. Back and forward. It helped him disperse the cold but didn't do a thing for his fear. It was a living, breathing thing, pushing at his chest, his mind.

Hours passed, and Kiran had no idea what time it was, whether it was day or night. Then, finally, he heard footsteps. The bolt shot on the door and a man stood there.

"You will be tried for their murder this afternoon."

Anger swelled inside Kiran. He hadn't killed them. A growl started in his mind and suddenly pain overtook him. His body distorted, his mind screaming in agony. His bones stretched and reshaped, his face reforming then the pain disappeared. His senses sang with clarity, and the stench of the room made his stomach bubble with disgust. A horrified gasp drew his attention back to the man. He stood frozen in the doorway, and Kiran charged, a harsh growl of irritation echoing through the wall as he sprang.

He hit the door as it shut. He heard the panicked breaths of the man, the curses and the clang as the bolt shot home, trapping him inside the room once more.

"A tiger. A fuckin' tiger." The man's voice was audible through the door. His hurried footsteps signaled his departure.

Kiran prowled the room, frustrated by his failure to escape.

Ten minutes passed and Kiran heard footsteps again. He tensed, his muscles bunching. The door flew open, bright lights blinded him before he could spring at the enemy. A gun fired. He felt a second of pain before he started swaying. Blackness followed and with it a soul-deep terror. Monsters stalked his mind. Everywhere he looked, they were there. They sliced his flesh, his frantic attempts to avoid them useless. Pain battled with fear. Hopelessness assailed him. A scream formed in his throat, the force of it burning his throat.

"Kiran. Kiran."

His eyes flew open, his body ready to spring into flight mode.

"Kiran, it's Rohan. You were shouting in your sleep. Growling. You okay?"

"A dream?" Kiran sat up and checked all corners of the room before swiping his hand over his hand. His rigid form relaxed slowly. A dream. It had all been a dream, yet it had seemed so real. "I'm sorry I woke you."

"No problem." Rohan's warm arms came around him, tugging him back to a reclining position. Kiran fell against Rohan, his heart still pounding with remembered fear. Had it been a dream? Or had the accusations been right and he'd really murdered three people? He swallowed and forced his thoughts to sex. He didn't know if Rohan could read his mind all the time, and he wasn't ready to talk about the dream yet. It would be best if he kept this to himself while he thought about it and what the dream meant.

Two Weeks Later

Nando's girlfriend informed David that Nando had gone to New Zealand on business. When pushed she'd admitted Nando rang her every few days and he was currently in the South Island. Blackmail gained him all sorts of information, and David wasn't afraid to use every method at his disposal if it helped him learn the fate of his beloved slave.

His inquiries at the house had produced a concoction of weird stories about screaming men and the roar of tigers in the middle of the night. And blood. One servant swore that blood flowed across the tiled floor of one of the slaves' common rooms. David wasn't sure what to make of that tale since the servant seemed to spin into madness, sometimes lucid. Sometimes not.

He'd checked again for the tracking beacon he'd planted at the back of his slave's neck but found no sign of life. It was as if his slave had vanished off the face of the Earth.

The plane touched down in Christchurch. Fatigue ate at David, slumping his shoulders and making him feel every one of his forty-five years. Despite wanting to start his search for Nando, rest was necessary. He'd asked his secretary to contact him once she knew of Nando's most recent location. He'd book into a hotel and recuperate while he waited.

When Nando hit Christchurch, the tracker unit started beeping. Nando turned the rental onto the shoulder of the road and grabbed it off the passenger seat to check the location.

"About time!"

He scanned the unit and checked the map. South of Dunedin. A small town called Middlemarch. Perfect. Fewer witnesses in a small town. He could be in and out in a matter of hours, find Kiran and do the deed.

"I should have killed him in India. Done the job myself instead of delegating the task." Nando's words echoed in the interior of the car. He checked for traffic and pulled back onto the road, the nervous tension inside dispersed by newfound confidence.

No, he'd done everything right. He'd imprisoned Kiran and taken his opportunities as they'd come. At least now he could kill Kiran away from prying eyes at home. Kiran's death would appear a random murder, and he'd leave the country before the local cops had a chance to pin the death on him.

Perfect.

He'd go back to his life with no one the wiser.

"HE'S GOING TO MIDDLEMARCH," David's secretary said in her crisp voice. "It's a country town not far from Mosgiel. I've booked you a flight from Christchurch to Dunedin and organized a rental car. Nando is driving from Christchurch so you will arrive in Middlemarch before him."

"Thank you," David said. "Do we know why he's going to Middlemarch?"

"No. The girl doesn't know."

"Do you believe her?" David trusted his secretary's judgment and paid her accordingly.

"I believe she is telling the truth."

"So it's possible he might change his destination?"

"Possible, but according to the girlfriend, he sounded excited about reaching Middlemarch. Would you like me to book a room in Middlemarch for you?"

"No," David said slowly. "I think I'll try to locate him first so I can follow and observe. He won't be expecting me. I want you to find out where he's staying. Ask the girl to find out."

"She might balk at that," the secretary warned.

"Try," David ordered. "I will contact you at the same time tomorrow."

The next day he waited impatiently in Dunedin. Damn, he was tired of this chasing around the countryside searching for Nando. All he wanted was to learn the truth about Kiran. Although his gut told him Kiran was still alive, reality had to intrude. It hadn't taken long to learn about his youngest brother and the mask he wore for the family. It was possible Kiran was dead contrary to what his sources in India had told him.

Either way, his brother had to pay.

Nando must learn who was boss in the family, and where the power belonged.

His cell phone rang, and when he checked the screen, he saw it was the call he was waiting for from his secretary.

"He's staying at the Blackwood Hotel near the airport for tonight," his secretary said.

"How did you find out?"

"You don't want to know," his secretary replied.

"Remind me to give you a pay rise."

"You already pay me well," his secretary said. "I'm merely doing my job."

"Thank you." After disconnecting the call, David checked the tourist map he'd picked up and saw an ad for the Blackwood Hotel. A few minutes later he'd booked a room and was on his way to the hotel. While he waited in Dunedin, he thought of obtaining a disguise so his brother didn't recognize him straightaway. He'd sit in the lobby and wait for his brother's arrival. Or better yet, he'd find a way to unobtrusively watch the cars arriving. That way he could follow his brother to Middlemarch.

He considered that for a moment, tempted to confront his brother and end it all now. No. Probably best to save their confrontation for the smaller town. He'd done a little research on Middlemarch. It was famous for the Singles Ball held each year around April and as the starting point of the Otago rail trail. Apart from that, it was a typical country town with a dwindling population.

The perfect place for a meeting with his youngest brother.

KIRAN AND GAVIN STOPPED by the café for a quick coffee after inoculating two lots of calves and sewing up a horse's leg. The calves hadn't cooperated despite Kiran's reassurance, and they were both wearing splotches of mud on their clothing.

"We'd better sit outside in the garden," Gavin said. "You want your usual?"

Kiran nodded, giving Gavin a tired grin. Exhaustion clung to him like a limpet, yet his feline prowled his mind, restless and uneasy. He opened the gate leading to the café garden and dropped into one of the bench seats next to a wooden table, wondering if he dared to close his eyes and attempt sleep or if the dreams would come.

Again.

He'd dreamed every night for the last two weeks.

The same dream.

Every night he slid into the nightmare despite trying to stay awake. The dream ended in the same place, but Kiran had started to worry that maybe there was something bad in his past. Had he murdered those three people? In his dream he was convinced of his innocence.

Kiran blinked and shook his head, forcing his fatigue away to concentrate on his surroundings. Emily had a great place here. It soothed and welcomed. No wonder the café was doing so well.

Some sort of tree grew in the corner, offering shade to part of the garden. Purple and white petunias grew in wooden barrels while a small water feature offered a soothing background noise. Kiran closed his eyes, his senses reaching out. Immediately he sensed the mate bond. The presence of the bond soothed his agitated feline. He heard almost silent footfalls, and when he opened his eyes, Rohan stood in front of him.

"You okay?"

"Yes. No."

"So which is it?"

Kiran gave an irritable shrug. "Hell if I know."

"Did I tire you out last night?" Rohan dropped onto the seat beside him, and his proximity eased his twitchy feline.

"I'm tired, yeah. But this is something else. I'm on edge and I don't know why." He sucked in a deep breath, hoping to stave off a yawn. Instead he breathed Rohan's scent and it called to him. He leaned into his mate, craving the solid contact. *I'm dreaming every night.*

Why didn't you tell me? Rohan wrinkled his nose at the fragrant mud on Kiran. Kiran half expected Rohan to push him away, but he didn't. He drew Kiran closer and kissed him. He held Kiran's face and traced the fullness of his lips, exploring and openly showing his love. Kiran sank greedily into the kiss, his eyes closing as Rohan devoured him.

A polite cough pulled them out of the kiss. Dazed, Kiran's eyes fluttered open to see Gavin grinning at them.

"No wonder you're tired." Gavin's eyes widened suddenly. He scrutinized them closely and leaned over to sniff. A sudden smile wreathed his mouth. "Damn, the two of you have mated. Why didn't you say something?" He frowned. "I can't believe I didn't notice."

"Maybe it's because we're tiger. Ambar knows," Rohan said.

Emily arrived with a tray of coffee, and Kiran, who was closest, shot to his feet. He glanced over his shoulder before seizing the tray from Emily.

"Hell, Emily," he chided. "Do you want to get us in trouble with Saber? I heard him tell you off when I was out at your place last night helping with the stock."

"I'm pregnant, not helpless," she snapped. "Gavin, you have to tell him it's good for pregnant women to keep active. He won't let me do anything, and he has Tomasine and Isabella reporting to him. They think it's cute. I know they wouldn't like it if they were me," she added in a dark tone.

Gavin chuckled. "I tried to talk to him, Emily, but he loves you and he worries."

"Saber asked if you're still coming out to the house tonight," Emily said to Kiran. "I think he's gonna ring you, but something has come up and he had to go to Dunedin. He won't be home until around nine or ten tonight."

"I might come out anyway," Kiran said. "I can work with the calves tonight and get them used to leading."

"Can I come and help?" Rohan asked. "I've been curious about your training."

"Come for dinner," Emily said.

"Did you know Kiran and Rohan have mated?" Gavin asked.

"Really?" Emily hugged Kiran, heedless of the dirt on his clothes.

"Holy crap," Kiran said. He pushed Emily away and placed his hand on her rounded stomach. "You've got an active baby in there."

"It's a healthy baby," Gavin said.

"A soccer player," Kiran said with certainty, letting his hand drop to his side. "A boy by the smell of him."

"The baby hasn't cooperated when we've done our scans," Gavin said. "I haven't been able to tell what sex it is."

Emily clapped her hand over her ears. "We wanted it to be a surprise."

"Hell, all I can smell is the muck and mud you and Gavin are wearing," Rohan said.

"A boy?" Emily eased her hands away from her ears. Her hand rose to cover her belly in a protective manner. "Saber will be pleased. Still a pain in my butt though. His mother-hen act is driving me nuts."

"I'll protect you, Emily," Kiran said with a grin.

"We'll have a better idea at your next checkup," Gavin said. "Next week, right?"

"Yes." Emily groaned and wrinkled her nose. "As much as I'd like to fib, I can't do that to Saber. I'll probably tell him and suffer the extra-protective mode. We might be able to decide on a list of names now."

A small bus pulled up outside the café with a screech of brakes. The doors opened and passengers piled out.

"Oops, my cue to go," Emily said. "Dinner tonight at six," she said to Kiran and Rohan. "We'll talk about a party to celebrate your mating as well. It's about time we had a get-together."

"I'd better head back to the store," Rohan said. He gave Kiran a quick kiss and waved at Gavin. *I love you, Kiran.*

See you later. I can't wait to touch you again, feel your cock inside my mouth. Kiran smiled at the thought he sent whizzing to Rohan. The moment Rohan left, Kiran's uneasiness returned. "Do you feel uneasy when you're away from your mates?"

"Yes. It gets easier but the feeling never goes away, and when you're with your mate, or mates in my case, there's nothing better. I know this sounds corny but I feel whole."

Kiran nodded. It wasn't corny at all because Gavin had described exactly how he felt about Rohan. Rohan completed him.

"My dreams are getting worse. I'm having them every night." He described the blood and gore to Gavin. "There's something else I haven't mentioned. Since Rohan and I mated, we can communicate telepathically.

"Does he know about your dreams?"

"Not in detail. I've tried to keep it from him."

"Can you pluck thoughts from his head? Or my head?"

"Not with you," Kiran said. "It's only with Rohan. I can have a conversation with Rohan. I seem to have a better grasp on the mindreading than Rohan. He doesn't pick up my thoughts."

"Fascinating," Gavin said. "I've never heard of anything like that before. Let me know if there are developments."

"And the dreams?"

"I hate to say it but I think your memory is exerting itself. There could be an element of truth in your dreams."

Kiran snorted, trying to hide his fear. "Yeah, that's what I'm worried about."

THE CLOSER NANDO DROVE to Middlemarch, the stronger the tracking beacon glowed. It was almost six when he drove into the small town, his lip curling with disdain when he saw it. The town didn't boast a proper restaurant or hotel, merely some piddly bed and breakfasts. Not that he intended to stay a minute longer than he had to. Once he'd dealt with Kiran, he'd return to Dunedin and catch the first flight back to India. Maybe he'd go via Australia. Sydney presented some decadent treats for a tourist. No reason he couldn't enjoy himself before he returned home.

He glanced at the tracking unit. He'd driven past. Obviously he needed to turn down one of these side roads that seemed to lead into the hills and open country. The middle of nowhere.

That would be right.

Still, it would be best if no one saw him confront Kiran. Kill him.

ROHAN DROVE WITH ONE hand, his other clasped in Kiran's. "I can't wait to see you in action with the cattle."

Kiran snorted. "It's not that exciting."

"But I don't know anyone else who can do it."

"Yeah, communicating with animals still surprises the hell out of me. I'm surprised everyone has accepted it so well. The ones who know, I mean. If you could talk to animals, I'd think you were crazy."

"Just as well you're not me." Rohan kissed the back of Kiran's hand. "I'm in love with a man who talks to animals. And I love the way we can communicate privately."

"Yeah?"

"Yeah, it's like our own private version of phone sex."

They grinned at each other, though it was a trifle forced on Kiran's side. During the last couple of weeks, Rohan had told Kiran of his love. Kiran felt it, the strong ties between them, strengthened since they'd marked each other, but he couldn't stop worrying about the dreams. At the end of each workday, he couldn't wait to see Rohan again. He liked the way Ambar accepted him and made him feel like part of the Patel family. Most of all, he enjoyed climbing into bed with Rohan, sometimes making love, sometimes talking and holding each other. Yet despite all the pluses of his relationship, his past continued to gnaw at him. Something held him back from verbalizing his love to Rohan.

"It was great of Emily to invite us to dinner."

"I think Ambar was glad we were going out so she could entertain," Rohan said. "I'm trying not to act the heavy-handed brother."

"You're finding it hard because you take one look at Jake and know exactly what he has on his mind," Kiran said.

"He'd better not hurt her."

"Jake seems decent. We have to trust Ambar to make her own decisions. What?" he asked when Rohan shot him a quick look. "I think of Ambar as my sister, my family. I worry."

"She's a virgin." Rohan scowled. "Or at least I think she is. Aw, hell. I think we should go back home." He slowed the car.

"Ambar would kill both of us," Kiran said. "Besides, do you remember what it felt like when your parents tried to make your decisions for you?"

"Yeah, of course I—" Rohan broke off abruptly and picked up speed. He turned into the Mitchells' driveway before scowling at Kiran. "Okay. You've made your point. I'll try not to interfere or show my disapproval. Ambar doesn't have to do what I tell her. She's an adult."

"You're quick at this lesson stuff."

"Smartass." Rohan pulled up outside the Mitchells' sprawling homestead and switched off the ignition.

"Come on." Kiran climbed out of the car and strode up the path to the front door. The flower gardens lining the path were a blaze of red, white and blue. Kiran knocked on the door and opened it. "Emily! We're here," he shouted.

"I'm in the kitchen."

"Do you walk in like that all the time?" Rohan asked from behind him.

"I visit here a lot with Gavin. On the days Emily isn't working at the café we have morning tea here with Saber before we go on rounds." Kiran removed his boots and left them on the doorstep. Rohan followed suit. They closed the front door and made their way to the kitchen.

"That smells great, Emily," Kiran said, pausing to kiss her on the cheek. "How is the baby this evening?" A joint of roast beef rested on a board while the lids of pots jingled on the stovetop.

"Active," Emily said, placing one hand on the rounded swell of her stomach. "I can't believe I'm having a child after all this time. I'd almost given up on the baby front."

"You're going to make a great mother, Emily," Kiran said. He loved Emily like a sister and admired Saber. He enjoyed his visits out here to see them and was glad he could include Rohan this time.

"Thanks. I'm looking forward to our child's arrival. Saber's twin brothers Sly and Joe were a challenge, according to Saber. Felix and Leo back him up on that, although Sly and Joe deny it. I've rung Sly and Joe and told them we're organizing a party for your mating. You'll be able to meet them then."

"Won't a party be too much for you?" Rohan asked.

Emily grinned. "I'm not doing much, apart from inviting people. All our friends are bringing a supper plate, and if everyone brings their beverage of choice, I won't have to do much. Kiran, will you set the table for me? You know where everything is. There are beers in the fridge or some wine if you'd prefer. I'll have an orange juice."

Kiran moved into action, grabbing a tablecloth and cutlery. When he looked up, he saw Rohan watching him closely.

Nice arse.

You think? Kiran shot a swift look at Emily and winked back at Rohan. He put an extra wiggle in his walk when he went to grab the drinks from the fridge, smirking at Rohan's swift intake of air. The man was easy, and suddenly he couldn't wait to get back to their place for some private time.

That wasn't fair, Rohan thought.

Kiran smirked. *You started it.*

Emily carved the roast and slid slices of meat onto the heated plates. She added vegetables and handed the plates over to Kiran, who placed them on the table.

"When is Saber due home?" Rohan asked.

"Around nine," Emily said. "Why?"

"I thought I heard a car out front," Kiran said.

"Yeah, that's why I asked."

"I'm not expecting anyone else. Leo went with Saber because it was something to do with the vineyard."

A thump sounded on the front door.

"Do you want me to get it?" Kiran asked.

Emily placed a hand on his shoulder, stopping him from rising. "No stay there. You and Rohan start your dinner. I won't be long." She walked away, disappearing around the corner.

Another strident knock sounded on the door.

"They're impatient. Is it polite to say that she's started to waddle?" Rohan asked in a low voice.

"I wouldn't let Saber hear you say that. He's very protective. He'd probably want to know why you were staring at his wife's backside." Kiran mock frowned. "Hell, I want to know why you're staring at her butt."

"Looking and touching are different," Rohan said. "There's only one person I want to touch and that's you."

Kiran froze, his head cocking to hear better. A scream sounded. A loud thump. Kiran and Rohan jumped to their feet and raced from the kitchen.

They came face-to-face with a man holding a gun. Kiran kept moving, desperate to get to Emily. Where the hell was she? He couldn't see her. No shots. That was good.

"Stop or I'll shoot," the man snarled.

Rohan and Kiran came to a halt, shoulders touching, tension radiating between them.

"Back into that room." The gunman indicated the lounge behind them. "Back up slow and keep your hands where I can see them."

"Do you know him?" Rohan whispered.

The man waved his gun. "No talking."

I don't know him. Kiran continued to back away, moving in the direction the man told them to. He didn't recognize him, although the man, like them, was from India. But what the hell was he doing here and why was he holding them at gunpoint? *Did you see Emily?*

No. Concern puckered Rohan's forehead.

"Sit."

Rohan and Kiran took a seat each, instinctively putting space between them instead of sitting on the couch. If the man decided to shoot, he couldn't shoot both of them easily, giving one a chance to escape.

Despite listening hard, he couldn't hear Emily. Damn, they had to do something. Fast.

"What do you want?" Kiran demanded. *We need to distract him.*

How? "Who the hell are you?" Rohan asked.

The man didn't take his gaze off Kiran. Something, a memory, stirred at the back of Kiran's mind but it dissolved before he could grasp and make sense of it. *We'll jump him.*

The man laughed, an unpleasant sound that grated on Kiran's nerves. *Emily.* Damn, Saber would kill him if anything happened to her. They had to overpower the man, get rid of the gun. He glanced at Rohan, received an imperceptible nod. Rohan was ready.

"Do you know who I am?" the man asked, his attention focused on Kiran. "I've been searching for you. I couldn't believe it when I saw you get out of that vehicle."

"Should I?"

The man narrowed his eyes, a glint of emotion flickering before it went cold. "My feelings are hurt. I came all this way and you don't remember me."

Kiran focused on his face and studied it. Really studied it. The man's eyes. Something about him did look familiar. Where? Kiran's breath hissed out when he clicked. He looked like the man in his dream—the dream he'd had recently. Kiran shrugged. "And here I didn't think I was very important."

"How did you escape the zoo?"

Kiran's eyes narrowed. "You sent me there?" He inhaled, testing the man's scent and couldn't smell feline. The man was a human, which gave them an advantage.

"No, my men did. I'm here to clean up the mess."

"What do you want?" Kiran stood, tired of pissing around. "Rohan, go and check on Emily."

"Stay where you are," the man snapped. The gun wavered. Kiran caught a trace of fear in his voice.

Rohan sprang from his seat and was halfway across the room when the man pulled the trigger. The shot echoed in the lounge. Rohan staggered, fell. Kiran's yell of horror rang out, fury striking seconds later. He jumped the man, his greater bulk sending them both flying. They hit the floor hard, Kiran's head thudding against the wooden coffee table. Despite the wave of dizziness, he held tight, grappling for the gun, bending the man's wrist cruelly. A bone cracked and the gun slipped from the man's hand. A shot fired from behind. Blood bloomed on the man's chest and he stilled.

Kiran leapt to his feet and whirled around, his head pounding. The scent of sandalwood reached him, his nose wrinkling in distaste.

A familiar figure. Tall. Strong. Long, dark hair slicked back and fastened at his nape. A smart charcoal gray suit. A picture of elegance and beauty.

A man with a distinctly cruel side. Memories ripped holes in his mind.

Blood. *So much blood*.

"You're alive," the man said.

His master stood in the doorway, gun extended, an expression of satisfaction on his face. He flicked the safety and placed the gun inside his suit jacket pocket. For an instant Kiran faltered, mired in the horror of his past, then a soft masculine groan yanked him back to the present. He didn't owe this man a thing because he'd repaid his debts tenfold during the last fifteen years. Rohan was his future, and it took seeing this man to make Kiran realize he'd received a second chance.

He scrambled to his mate's side, ignoring the throb in his head. A mere lump. He'd probably have a headache for a few hours, but it was bearable. "Hell, Rohan. You okay?"

"Arm hurts like fuck," Rohan muttered. "I'm okay. Go and check on Emily."

"Can you manage a shift?" Kiran asked in a terse voice, already heading from the room in search of Emily. "That will help." Memories continued to pour back. Small and large. Time for that later. Kiran brushed past the master, intent on helping Emily.

David's hand flashed out to halt Kiran's progress. "Is that all the greeting I receive?"

"I have to see to my friend." Kiran yanked from his touch, his skin crawling. It brought back memories. Of deprivation. Of numerous lashes. Of blood.

Death.

Emily. He had to focus on Emily.

"Emily!" Kiran saw her prone body as soon as he entered the passage. She lay motionless on the floor, facedown. He crouched at her side. "Emily? Emily? Are you awake?" Swallowing his fear, he checked her pulse. He found one. Not a strong one, but at least she was alive. The scent of blood. He rolled her gently and found a lump on her head. It bled sluggishly. Then he saw the pool of blood spreading between her legs.

"Shit."

"Kiran, it's time to go home. I've come to take you home to India."

Kiran ignored the master. "Rohan! Rohan?"

A tiger appeared from the lounge. The master gasped and backed up, almost tripping over Kiran and Emily.

"Watch it!" Kiran snapped. "Stand over there and don't move."

"Don't speak to me like that." The steely tones held reprimand. Once Kiran would have cringed, terrified of the punishment in store for him. Too bad he didn't care anymore.

Kiran ignored the master. "Rohan, ring Gavin and tell him it's an emergency. Emily's bleeding and it doesn't look good. I think she's losing the baby."

Emily moaned, claiming his attention. "Emily, love. It's okay. No don't move. Gavin is on his way." At least

226

he hoped Gavin could come immediately and wasn't on another call. Emily's eyelids fluttered and her eyes opened.

"The baby?" Her eyes beseeched him to tell her everything would be all right. Kiran swallowed, knowing things didn't look good. "Kiran!" Emily tensed, lines of pain contorting her face.

He took her hand, barely wincing when her fingernails dug into his palm. "Hang tight, Emily. Gavin will be here soon." She squeezed his hand, her body arching upward before she relaxed. A tear leaked from the corner of her eye.

The lump in Kiran's throat grew to epic proportions. He felt so helpless.

"I insist we leave now," David said. "You don't owe these people anything. Come home with me. Now." The steel in the last word was unmistakable.

"Fuck off," Kiran snarled. "I don't owe you a thing."

"I saved you from the streets. I fed you, clothed you. I love you," David said, moving away from the wall, but not before he glanced at the far end of the passage.

Love?

Kiran laughed at the irony. The man wouldn't know real love if it bit him on the butt. "You might have taken me off the streets, but my life didn't improve."

"You know this man, Kiran?" Rohan joined Kiran. "Gavin is on his way. About ten minutes he said. I asked him to bring Charlie." His expression told Kiran that Rohan had mentioned the gun and the fact one of the gunmen was still here. Good.

Kiran shot a glance at David, his former master before turning his attention back to Emily. "I hope they drive fast." He and Rohan shared a quick glance, and the love in that one look soothed some of Kiran's apprehension. *You okay?*

Yeah. "The bullet popped out when I shifted," he murmured so the other man wouldn't hear. "It still hurts but the flesh has started to knit together. I was so rattled I didn't think of shifting."

"You can thank Gavin," Kiran said. "In the weeks I've worked with him I've learned a lot."

"If you don't come with me now, I will shoot both of your friends," David said in a hard voice.

Both he and Rohan looked up. Emily moaned, the sound full of pain, but David claimed their attention with the gun pointed at them.

Kiran and Rohan both heard the car at the same time. David didn't hear it, his attention remaining on them, the gun held level and with confidence.

Time to get this show on the road. He only hoped the ugly truth didn't send Rohan fleeing.

Kiran stood slowly, not wanting to panic David. "All right. I'll come with you now. There's no need to involve these people. You're right. I owe you my allegiance."

"You owe me, love," David snapped. "I made sure you were educated, always had protection."

Shit. It had been different before. His options had been limited. Every time he'd shown a bit of independence someone had beat it out of him. Drugged him to keep him calm. Was it any wonder he'd blindly followed every order? Allowed his master to fuck him and fucked others on demand? Kiran forced his agitated feline to the back of his mind, imprisoning him. The feline snarled, disliking the need for a cage.

Kiran dredged up the shell of his former self, silently protesting the uncomfortable fit. Didn't matter. He'd do anything to save Emily and Rohan. *Rohan, back up. Let him think I'm going to go with him.*

Damn, you can't go with him. He's unstable.

When he looked up, his gaze skittered over the master's face. His head bowed. "I'm sorry, master. You are right. I owe you much. I will leave with you whenever you are ready."

You are not going with him!

Kiran could feel Rohan's confusion battering him and knew if he looked at his mate, he'd lose it. He concentrated on David, drawing his attention away from the others and hopefully Charlie and Gavin's arrival. Yeah, David. The man was *not* his master.

"I don't believe you," David said. "Why didn't you come home before?"

"Because I didn't remember. I didn't know anything about my past. All I knew was my name."

David gestured with the gun, pointing it toward Rohan. "Is this true?"

"Yes." Rohan frowned at Kiran. "When did you remember? Why didn't you tell us?"

"Nando's face seemed familiar, and it all came back to me just now."

David nodded thoughtfully. "So you didn't contact me, you didn't search for me because you didn't remember?"

"Yes," Kiran said, trying to ignore Emily's pain. The less he said the better. He didn't want David to suspect his lies. Even if he'd had his memory, he wouldn't have returned. The only way he'd resume his former life was under coercion. He heard cautious footsteps outside and kept talking, wanting to distract, to keep David's attention firmly on him. "Put the gun down. Let my friends go. Emily needs medical attention. I'll come with you. Please, just let my friends go."

"I don't believe you're telling the truth." David kept the gun pointed at Rohan.

Kiran noticed with approval the way Rohan kept his body between Emily and David.

"Put the gun down," Charlie appeared at the end of the passage, weapon drawn.

Emily moaned, and Rohan turned, bending to murmur reassurance to her.

"We've got the house surrounded. Put the gun down," Laura, the other Middlemarch cop demanded.

With his attention on David, Kiran noticed the shift in the man's focus and leapt at him. He drove low, knocking David into the wall with a loud thump. A weapon fired, the stench of powder filling the air. A curse sounded, but Kiran didn't release David. He gripped his forearms, pinning him in place, aware of running feet, shouts and through it, Gavin's clear and calm directions.

"We've got him, Kiran," Charlie said.

Kiran eased up on the pressure and waited until Laura snapped a pair of handcuffs on David. "Did anyone get hit?"

"You're making a mistake," David protested. "I haven't done anything. Ask, Kiran. He'll tell you."

"You'll find a body in the lounge," Kiran said. "He shot the man. They're brothers."

"Kiran!" Panic sounded in David's voice as he realized Kiran didn't intend to help him. "I love you. You can't do this to me."

Something broke in Kiran and he turned to David with a snarl, not bothering to hide the tiger pushing for freedom in front of him. "You're a cruel, vicious man who gets off on power. You might have provided me with food and shelter, taken me off the streets, but you did it because it suited you." He pushed his face close, his voice guttural because of his protruding canines. "You enslaved me and others using us like disposable toys. That's not love. That's abuse of power, preying on the weak. I hope you damn well rot in jail."

Kiran pushed away in disgust and strode away to check on Emily. He had new friends, a job to do and a mate who loved him. Time to live for the future.

Chapter Ten

"Where's Gavin?"

"He's in Emily and Saber's bedroom," Rohan said.

Kiran headed down the other end of the passage, his heart kicking with panic when he heard Emily's heartwrenching cries. He tapped briefly on the door and stepped inside. "What can I do?"

"Hold Emily's hand while I check the bleeding," Gavin said in a terse voice.

Kiran took one look at his face and knew the news wasn't good. Gavin rifled through his bag and grabbed several items while Kiran concentrated on Emily.

"My baby," she sobbed. "My baby isn't moving. He pushed me. Kicked me." Tears ran down her face, the sight wrenching at his heart.

Another look at Gavin told him the truth.

The baby was dead.

Hell, this was his fault.

"I'm so sorry, Emily." He didn't make the mistake of telling her there would be other babies. That wouldn't help right now while she was grieving. "This is my fault. They wanted to get to me."

Emily's hand tightened in his, her eyes full of torment. "You didn't do this. That man did. Not your fault."

"Okay, Emily. I have the bleeding under control now," Gavin said. "I'm going to give you something to help you sleep."

"Saber?" Emily asked, gripping Kiran's hand so hard her nails dug into his palm. "What about the baby?"

"Saber is on his way home," Gavin said. "By the time you wake up, he'll be home. I'll do tests soon and we'll talk."

"I'll stay with you until you fall asleep," Kiran said. It was the least he could do.

Gavin nodded. "I'll be back in a minute." He opened the door and a tiger stood there.

Kiran, that bloody man put a bullet in my arse and it didn't come out when I shifted. Irritation sounded in Rohan.

"Gavin, you have another patient. Rohan was shot."

"Where?" Gavin said, scanning Rohan.

Kiran's lips twitched. "His butt. You might want to take a look at his arm as well. He was shot earlier. Shifting seemed to help the first time."

"Why didn't you say something?" Gavin strode through the doorway. "Let's leave Emily alone with Kiran. I'll take a quick look in the next room."

The door closed behind them. Emily's breathing was quiet, her eyes closed. Kiran continued to hold her hand, wondering how he could have done things differently, how he could have kept both Emily and Rohan safe. The baby. Time passed and Emily slept.

In the short time he'd known Emily, he'd come to care for her. She was the heart of the Mitchell family. Everyone loved her, and Kiran didn't know how they'd get past this.

He heard the distant sound of a car, determined footsteps and the door flew open. The raw pain on Saber's face tore at Kiran's gut.

"She's asleep," Kiran said.

"But she's okay?"

"Yeah." Kiran hesitated to mention the baby. He wasn't sure of the details yet, but he knew the baby hadn't moved since Emily had fallen.

Saber sat on the edge of the bed opposite Kiran. He brushed her hair away from her face in a tender gesture that made Kiran feel in the way.

"Saber?"

"I'm here, kitten."

Kiran released her hand and stood.

"The others are in the kitchen," Saber said.

Kiran nodded.

"Saber, the baby. It's not moving," Emily said, a tearful catch in her voice. "I think he's died. Gavin said he'll have to do more tests. I fell." Pain choked her up. "There was so much blood."

Kiran slipped from the room, the agony of Emily's words echoing through his mind. As he closed the door, he heard the murmur of Saber's reply and his guilt intensified.

If it hadn't been for him, David and Nando wouldn't have come to Middlemarch.

He entered the kitchen, and Charlie arrived seconds later.

"How's Emily?" Gavin asked.

"She woke just as I left. I left her with Saber. Is the baby dead?"

Gavin dragged a hand through his hair, looking tired. "I think...yeah, it is. I couldn't hear a heartbeat. I'll do more tests and operate if necessary tomorrow."

"Shit," Kiran said, feeling sick with dread. *His fault.*

"Feel up to answering some questions?" Charlie asked. "We can go into one of the other rooms."

"Here is fine. I don't mind." Kiran dropped into a chair near Rohan, the need for Rohan's touch roaring through him. "You okay?"

Rohan snorted. "See how you feel having a bullet dug out of your butt. It's sore."

"I'm sorry," Kiran said.

"What have you got to be sorry for? You didn't shoot me." Rohan stood and moved gingerly. "Damn, it's hard to sit. Don't smirk," Rohan said to Gavin and Charlie. "I'll unsheathe my claws in your rear ends and see how easy it is for you to sit on a wooden chair."

Kiran lifted his shoulders in an irritable shrug. "Yeah, but it was because of me you were shot and Emily was hurt."

"Rubbish," Rohan said, moving to stand behind Kiran. Rohan grasped his shoulder and squeezed in silent support. Rohan's touch helped bolster his dragging spirits.

Damn, he'd never felt so drained in all his life. He should be happy considering his memory had returned, but the knowledge of his past made things worse.

Gavin handed him a drink. "Here, get that in you. Rohan said your memory has come back."

"Yeah."

"And those guys?" Charlie asked.

Kiran's hand clenched around the glass. "It's not pretty. Are you sure you want to hear?"

"I'm going to have to do a report of some sort," Charlie said. "We have one dead and another in our jail. Laura wasn't happy about babysitting the man. She said he's rude and obnoxious. She was tempted to kick his butt but couldn't because that would be police brutality." Charlie shook his head, his eyes crinkling at the corners in a trace of amusement.

"I'm in the country without visas or paperwork," Kiran said. "If I'm in a report, that will raise questions."

"Don't worry about the paperwork," Saber said entering the kitchen. "We can sort that out for you quick enough. We have contacts."

Kiran swallowed, the black of depression gnawing at his conscience. His fault. *All his fault.* "Why would you do that for me when my presence brought David and Nando to Middlemarch? It's because of me they hurt Emily."

"And it's because of me they tracked you here. I kept meaning to take the chip into Charlie and Laura, but I've had a lot on my mind and forgot," Saber said in a hard voice. "If anyone is at fault it's me."

"Bullshit," Gavin said. "You're both forgetting those men were driven and intent on getting to Kiran. From what Rohan said, neither of them intended to leave without Kiran. You have to accept there are some things in life we can't change. All we can do is hang tight and ride the storm. It could have been a lot worse. Emily will get through this. She's healthy and there's no reason she can't have children in the future. Rohan is already healing and Kiran has his memory back." Gavin pulled out a chair and shunted it toward Saber. "Sit. You must have driven like a maniac to get back so soon."

"I was halfway home when you rang," Saber said, his eyes glittering with unshed tears. "I had a bad feeling and left Leo to deal with the meeting." Saber took the whisky Gavin handed him and turned to Kiran. "I want to know why they were here. Talk quick so I can go back and sit with Emily."

Fear compressed Kiran's throat and weighted his chest. A sliver of panic shot through him. They'd never look at him the same after hearing about his sordid past.

"Kiran." Rohan pulled up a chair and sat beside Kiran, wincing a little and shifting to find a comfortable spot. Rohan took his hand and gripped it tight.

It was Rohan's silent comfort that gave Kiran the impetus he needed to start.

"I lived on the streets in Mumbai. A lot of kids do. I never knew who my father was but my mother worked as an extra in films. She died when I was about eight. When I turned ten, the local authorities cleared the derelict buildings we lived in to make way for new luxury housing.

I was bigger than the others and attracted attention. David came to see the kids they'd captured and took me and several others to his house. He keeps a...I guess you could call it a harem. He educates and grooms children. Some of them he chooses to take to his bed once they turn eighteen. I was his favorite sexual slave." Kiran paused, looked down at his hands, unable to meet the gazes of the men he'd come to view as friends. He didn't want to see their expressions of disgust. Distaste. His throat and mouth felt dry and he took a quick sip of whisky. "David was into kinky stuff. We called him the master and anyone who crossed him died. We all became used to seeing slaves die, seeing the blood. It was a powerful incentive to do whatever he asked. If he asked us to fuck someone, we did it. They used to drug us to keep us in line and make us easier to manage."

"But I don't understand. You're a tiger shifter," Charlie said. "Couldn't you have escaped?"

"I didn't know I was a shifter," Kiran said. "Remember, I didn't know my father, and my mother never said anything. David used to go away on frequent business trips. He had several brothers. They were lazy drunkards who didn't work, apart from Nando, the youngest. David went away on business and Nando had friends over. I was in the wrong place at the wrong time and overheard them talking. They wanted to get rid of David, and Nando would take over the family business. They caught me eavesdropping and set me up. I woke up in a room with three dead servants.

He shivered as he remembered the scene. "There was blood everywhere. A knife with my fingerprints on the handle. Nando accused me of murder, and they locked me up. I was scared and angry. I'm not sure what happened, but I guess it pushed my feline to the surface because I knew I was going to die. I shifted, and when Nando's men opened the room, they found a tiger. Nando didn't know what was going on, but his men sold me in tiger form, and I ended up in the Auckland Zoo. I don't know what happened between the house in Mumbai and the zoo, but I woke with no memory of my past."

"Probably a mixture of drugs," Gavin said.

"They must have fit you with the tracking device at that stage," Saber said.

"No, the master fit all the slaves with tracking devices when he took them into his house. I've always had it, and obviously the shifting aggravated the site, which is why I noticed it."

"Nando must have worried when the tiger disappeared," Rohan added.

"He didn't know his men had sold me at first. When he found out he came to kill me. Clean up the mess, he said." Kiran pushed his whisky away and stood, releasing Rohan's hand. "That's the highlights. I'll go now."

"Where?" Saber said, standing to face him. "More importantly why?"

"But don't you want me to go? I keep telling you this is my fault. You've all made me feel so welcome. I don't want to cause more trouble."

"We're mates," Rohan said in a taut voice, a sense of betrayal flashing in his eyes. "You'd walk away and consign us both to hell?"

Kiran literally felt a physical wrench at the thought of parting from Rohan. He couldn't look at his mate. "I knew this was a bad idea." He walked toward the door, forcing his legs to move.

"Fuck you," Rohan snapped. "I'm not letting you walk away from something good. I love you. We're mates."

"Kiran." Saber's voice held command.

Slowly Kiran turned back. He saw determination. Friendship. Acceptance and love on their faces. Not a shred of the contempt he'd feared was in evidence.

"We all have things in our past we regret," Rohan said. "You were a kid. You had your choices taken from you and did what you needed to survive. I think you've turned out well. Stay. I can't face the thought of a life without you."

"You're a valuable part of our community," Saber said. "It's your choice to leave if you wish, but we'd like you to stay. We'll help you get papers and get through the official hurdles. Charlie and Laura will take care of the statement. All you need to do is sign it. You are not responsible for the actions of these two men."

"No problem," Charlie said. "It looks to me like a straightforward family squabble. The older brother keeps babbling about seeing a tiger. They'll want a report as to his state of mind."

The tight bands of tension inside Kiran released and his shoulders relaxed. He didn't want to leave Middlemarch or Rohan. This really was home. Hearing Saber and Charlie's easy acceptance went a long way to easing his guilt. And Rohan—Rohan loved him. "I guess I'm staying then."

"Great," Gavin said, his smile flashing as he winked at Charlie. "We might get that belated honeymoon in Samoa if I can train Kiran fast enough."

They all chuckled before Saber returned to Emily and Gavin went with him to check on her before leaving with Charlie.

"You ready to go home?" Rohan asked.

Kiran nodded, and they walked out to the SUV together.

"Hell of a day," Rohan said.

An understatement. His muscles ached as if he'd gone a few rounds in a boxing ring. "Yeah."

Rohan's eyes gleamed as he glanced at Kiran. "I vote we forget about eating and head straight to bed."

Fifteen minutes later, they entered their bedroom, closing the door on the rest of the world.

"Ambar's not home. Do you think things are serious between her and Jake?" Kiran asked.

"I'm more worried about us," Rohan answered. "Are we okay? You're not gonna leave?"

Kiran turned to face Rohan. "Only if you want me to."

"I can't see that happening. You're my mate. I can't imagine my life without you in it. I know things happened quickly between us, but I do love you."

"Show me."

"Strip." The harsh order in Rohan's voice sent a ripple of excitement through Kiran. He paused to wonder about the strangeness of that, how he could enjoy Rohan ordering him around in the bedroom yet hate it so much with David. He pushed aside the thought and concentrated on disrobing as quickly as possible.

"How is your butt?"

"You tell me." Fully naked, Rohan turned and flashed his arse in Kiran's direction.

"Nice," Kiran purred. "Very sexy."

"That's a given." Rohan grinned over his shoulder. "I'm talking about the bullet hole."

"It's healing well. I guess the shifting helped. It looks red but all the edges have knit together. You'll probably have a bit of a scar. Sexy."

"By tomorrow it should feel better. Maybe we could fit in a run tomorrow night after work. Gavin said shifting will speed the healing process. But meantime I have other things on my mind. On the bed. On your hands and knees."

Excitement filled Kiran as he hurried to obey. His cock stirred, his heart pumping with a rush of joy. Rohan was right. Them. Together. It was kismet.

"I love you, Kiran," Rohan said, moving on the bed behind him. His hands reached around to stroke Kiran's shaft.

"Damn it feels good when you touch me."

"Remember that. I like to touch you. The sex is great, but most of all, I love spending time with you. I love you, the good and bad." Rohan dropped a kiss on his shoulder and licked across an old scar. He stroked and used his thumb to tease the head of Kiran's cock. His left hand cupped his balls, gently rolling them while his mouth and tongue licked closer and closer to Kiran's mark. He started to tremble. "Hold on. Don't come yet."

Kiran groaned. "You need to move faster if you expect me to hold back."

Rohan released his cock and balls and started to grope his ass. Kiran widened his stance, biting his bottom lip to hold back his pleas for speed. He knew from experience Rohan loved to tease him. If he knew how desperate Kiran was to fuck, he'd take even longer to get to the good stuff. A finger stroked his pucker, wakening sensitive nerve endings and making them sing with jolts of pleasure. Rohan kissed one butt cheek and started to prepare him. Kiran knew it wouldn't take long. He shivered, his body jerking, emotions soaring. He loved Rohan so much, loved everything about the man.

Kiran's breath caught. It could have been the sharp jolt of pleasure when Rohan stroked across his gland or the chill of lube but Kiran knew better. He'd allowed himself to freely acknowledge what he felt for Rohan. The words trembled at the tip of his tongue ready to spill free.

Rohan moved again and Kiran felt the pressure of Rohan's cock tunneling into his ass. He groaned at the intrusion, savoring the faint bite of pain and the sweet swell of pleasure. Kiran pushed back against Rohan. He felt Rohan's breath caress his shoulder, felt warmed both inside and out. They rocked together, gradually increasing in speed until the scent of sex filled the air and their harsh breaths echoed through the room.

"Come for me now," Rohan said.

"Need a hand."

"My pleasure. Anything you want." Rohan's hand reached around his thigh and grasped his cock, pumping it vigorously in the exact way he liked while his mouth sought the marking site. At the warm rasp of his tongue, the pleasure spiked suddenly. Rohan drove deep and a white-hot conflagration gripped Kiran. He shuddered, his dick spasming, ecstasy charging through him. Slowly he came down from the high and realized Rohan was still hard. He tensed his backside and heat blossomed in him again. Rohan released his cock and gripped Kiran's shoulders, bending over him to suck on the mark at his shoulder. Rohan's hips slammed against Kiran's backside then stilled. He was vaguely aware of Rohan coming, his own cock twitching after Rohan sucked on his mark again.

Rohan made a purring sound of approval. He pulled from Kiran and rolled them over so they spooned. He gripped Kiran's cock and stroked until he came again, playing him like a maestro.

Gradually their breathing evened out. They were both a sticky mess and needed to clean up, but there was something Kiran wanted to do first. He turned in Rohan's arms so they were face-to-face. Kiran cupped Rohan's face.

Rohan smiled. "What?"

"I love you."

Rohan's eyes closed for an instant as if he were holding the thought close to his heart. When he opened his eyes again, his smile widened to flash his white teeth. "About time you realized it."

"So shoot me. I'm a slow learner."

"Nothing wrong with being a slow learner," Rohan said in a gentle voice. "It's the lesson learned that counts. I love you too, but I think you know that. You want to shower?"

"Yeah." Kiran rolled off the bed and they walked into the bathroom together. A sense of lightness and freedom filled Kiran. A sense of rightness, of belonging. He was right where he needed to be in Middlemarch with Rohan and the friends he'd made. The boy who'd lived on the streets had found a home, he'd found love. He'd found a mate. Best of all, he had a future to look forward to, and he couldn't wait to see how it unfolded with his mate at his side.

BONUS CHAPTER

STORM IN A TEACUP CAFÉ, MIDDLEMARCH, NEW ZEALAND

FELINE SHAPESHIFTER COUNCIL MEETING.

Present: Sid Blackburn, Agnes Paisley, Valerie McClintock, Benjamin Urquart, London Allbright

Apologies: Saber Mitchell

Her first Feline council meeting. London Allbright sucked in a fortifying breath as she maneuvered past a stroller and dodged a laughing toddler intent on escape. Emily Mitchell had encouraged her to accept the post when London had hesitated, telling her that the humans mated to shifters needed to stand up for themselves. This offer of a seat on the council was an honor, even if they required her to work hard in exchange.

"Ah, London." Sid Blackburn smiled at her and gestured at an empty seat. "We know you're busy, stepping in for Emily, and won't keep you for long."

Agnes reached over and patted London's hand, her expression etched with sorrow. "How is Emily, dear?"

"Saber said she's sleeping a lot. Gavin says she is healing and needs time." Every time she talked to Emily, her friend cried, although she didn't mention this. Truth was—London wanted to howl along with her. She kept thinking of Jenny, her sister who was murdered, and this, along with Emily's grief, kept shoving her off-balance.

"It's a terrible thing to lose a child at any time," Valerie said. "But this..." She trailed off, shaking her head, her eyes glittering with tears behind her glasses lenses.

Ben picked up his coffee. "Young Kiran is blaming himself. No one could have predicted this outcome."

London placed her tablet on the tabletop. She hid her hands in her lap, clenching and unclenching her fingers, willing herself not to cry. The café had been a somber place for the past two weeks.

"We'd better get this meeting underway," Ben said. "I need to shift my sheep this afternoon."

Agnes pulled a notebook from her handbag, opened it and scanned the contents. "We had intended to discuss the Halloween promotion."

Sid frowned. "Emily has been helping us with this."

London tapped a button on her tablet. "She gave me her notes and ideas. At least, Saber gave them to me. I've had a quick look and I think it will be enough for us to start planning the promotion."

"You have the floor, lass," Sid said and smiled in encouragement.

Agnes nodded in approval. "I do love an organized person."

"I discussed and brainstormed some of this with Emily before..." She swallowed, shook her head. "We thought a three-day event would work best. Run the promotion over a weekend—Friday, Saturday and Sunday. Early on the Friday night, we'd hold a trick or treat hour for the younger children. They can dress up in costumes. We'd ask the businesses and residents who live in the town to arrange treats or tricks for the kids. On Friday, Saturday, and Sunday nights, we'd open the haunted house from nine at night."

"That's late," Ben said.

"It's not dark until late. Nine might be too early. We need darkness to make the most of the special effects we're planning. Emily arranged the Mitchell twins—Joe and Sly—to help since she said they had some great ideas. We'll have the house set up for the Thursday night so we can wander through and iron out any kinks in the process."

Valerie wrinkled her nose. "I'm not sure I want to put myself at the mercy of those twins."

Ben guffawed, his green eyes twinkling. "Go on, Valerie. Live a little."

"Humph," Agnes said, also frowning. "I think payback might feature. Give an inch with those two scallywags and they grasp a mile or two."

"I think it would be good for the rest of the community to see us taking part," Sid commented. "We can build on the goodwill generated by the upcoming picnic."

London nodded. "The more the locals see you taking part, the better. It sends a message to the children and teenagers and fosters a sense of community. We could ask the local kids to do a walk through during the daylight on the Thursday. Offer this as a treat to those who win one of the events at the community picnic."

"Won't they'll tell everyone what to expect?" Ben asked.

"No," London said. "Not if we pitch this as a special surprise behind-the-scenes tour. We could even make it official and get them to sign a certificate to say they can't discuss anything in the house until Monday. I could type up official scare certificates. We could give them a T-shirt as part of their prize. Actually, we need judges for the best decorated shop or house. They could help with that too."

"I like it," Valerie said. "What else?"

London glanced at her tablet. "The café is having a special menu with graveyard cupcakes, eyeball cookies, mummy sausages. Stuff like that. Gerard and Henry said they could set up a sound system for the weekend, so music will play out on the street. We can set the scene with scary music. Megan Saxon said she'd man an apple dunking booth. Isabella suggested facepainting. She said that she would arrange several people to help with that." She checked her list again. "Saber said you'd discussed graveyard tours, but he thought you should keep that in reserve for another time and concentrate on the haunted house."

Agnes tapped a pen on the tabletop. "I can't get my mind off Joe and Sly in charge of the haunted house. Are we sure this is a good idea?"

London tried to bite back her laugh but it escaped in a gurgle. "They said you'd say that. Henry and Gerard are helping, and Jacey promised his aid as well. Emily had mentioned inviting Ambar Patel to volunteer."

Valerie let out a snort. "Emily is matchmaking again. I feel as if I should warn any woman who wanders within their sights."

"Now, now." Sid patted Valerie's hand. "The twins are mischievous but there is no malice in them. Look how well Saber, Felix and Leo turned out."

"I suppose we can live in hope," Agnes said with a sniff.

London, who had met the twins only briefly, couldn't wait to get to know them better. "Don't worry. I intend to supervise the entire process. We all want to do the best job we can. My suggestion is that we have a subcommittee to oversee the haunted house. I can report back to you regarding what we recommend, and you can make the final decisions. Would that work?"

The elders exchanged glances, then each of them nodded.

"Lass," Sid said. "That would be perfect. Give us each a task to help. I think we should meet weekly until the event."

"That works for me," Ben said. "How much are we charging for entrance?"

"I thought five dollars would be enough," London said. "Maybe a gold coin for children?"

"We should make a profit," Agnes declared.

"We have a healthy balance in the Feline council account," Sid said. "Why don't we aim to cover our costs and leave it at that?"

"As long as we cover costs," Valerie agreed. "That sounds fair."

"Is that everything?" Ben asked. "My sheep aren't mustering themselves."

"Away you go." Agnes made shooing motions with her right hand. "Sid, I presume you're going with Ben? Valerie, London and I will discuss the promotional posters and advertising, then adjourn until next week."

The two men left, and London jotted notes.

"Do you have time to design a poster?" Agnes asked.

"I can do it tonight." Now that young Ramsay was helping her with the baking at the café, she had more time to attend to her virtual assistant work.

"Thank you, dear," Valerie said as she stood. "If we are burdening you with too many tasks, please tell us. We don't want to scare you away."

"Was there anything else before we go?" Agnes asked.

"No. Truly, all I'm doing is following Emily's notes and organizing helpers. At the next meeting, I can give you a task each."

Agnes gave a brisk nod and stood. "Perfect."

London watched the two elderly women until they exited the café before heaving out a sigh of relief. That hadn't been too bad. Gerard had told her she'd be great. Henry, Jacey, and Megan had offered to help her with behind-the-scenes things. She grinned. They might regret that generosity.

A thought occurred, and she picked up her tablet and stood. After a quick glance around the café, she decided she had time to chat with Ramsay about preparing a Halloween menu.

She entered the kitchen and came to an abrupt halt. Emily stood at one work counter and was mixing a batch of cookies. Ramsay worked at the second counter and sneaked concerned glances at Emily as he rolled out dough for cheese scones.

"Emily, I thought you were taking the rest of the week off."

Emily swallowed and caught London's gaze. "I can't...I need...please, don't ring Saber." The large black shadows beneath her bloodshot eyes put years on her age. Pain rested on her features, her shoulders like a heavy weight. "I want to be busy so I can't think."

"I'll ring Saber, just to tell him that you're here. That's all." London came to a quick decision. "I was going to discuss a Halloween menu with Ramsay. If it's all right with you, I thought we'd plan a set-menu for the Friday and Saturday nights, plus do some themed cupcakes. We can find new recipes and test them or adapt some of our standard bakes. Ideas, Emily? Ramsay?"

"We can do the lemon slice and decorate it with eyeballs, spiders, black cats, pumpkins and things like that," Ramsay said.

Emily's cell phone rang. She stilled, then plucked it from her pocket. She thrust the phone at London. "Please."

London accepted the phone and walked toward the storeroom as she answered. "Saber, it's London. Emily is here at the café."

"Thank goodness," Saber said in a hoarse voice. "I panicked when she wasn't at home. I'll come and collect her."

"No! Please, I think she needs to keep busy. We're closing at five today. I'll bring her home once the café is closed."

"How is she?"

London heard the worry, the pain, the anguish in Saber's voice. "Not good. If I keep her busy then maybe she'll sleep better."

"I...okay. Call me if...if she needs me."

"I will. I promise."

"Thanks, London."

London hung up and rubbed the heel of her hand against her chest in an attempt to ease the tightness. Her eyes stung, and she knew it wouldn't take much for tears to spill over. She swallowed the scratchiness from her throat, straightened her shoulders, and marched back to join Emily and Ramsay.

Right. If Emily wanted busy, she'd give her busy. After all, they had a Halloween weekend to plan.

WANT MORE TIGERS?

Read Ambar's story, ***My Romantic Tangle***, the next Middlemarch Shifters adventure.

www.shelleymunro.com/books/my-romantic-tangle

ABOUT AUTHOR

USA Today bestselling author Shelley Munro lives in Auckland, the City of Sails, with her husband and a cheeky Jack Russell/mystery breed dog.

Typical New Zealanders, Shelley and her husband left home for their big OE soon after they married (translation of New Zealand speak - big overseas experience). A twelve-month-long adventure lengthened to six years of roaming the world. Enduring memories include being almost sat on by a mountain gorilla in Rwanda, lazing on white sandy beaches in India, whale watching in Alaska, searching for leprechauns in Ireland, and dealing with ghosts in an English pub.

While travel is still a big attraction, these days Shelley is most likely found in front of her computer following

SHELLEY MUNRO

another love - that of writing stories of contemporary and paranormal romance and adventure. Other interests include watching rugby (strictly for research purposes), cycling, playing croquet and the ukelele, and curling up with an enjoyable book.

Visit Shelley at her Website
www.shelleymunro.com

Join Shelley's Newsletter
www.shelleymunro.com/newsletter

ALSO BY SHELLEY

Paranormal

Middlemarch Shifters
My Scarlet Woman
My Younger Lover
My Peeping Tom
My Assassin
My Estranged Lover
My Feline Protector
My Determined Suitor
My Cat Burglar
My Stray Cat
My Second Chance
My Plan B
My Cat Nap
My Romantic Tangle
My Blue Lady

SHELLEY MUNRO

My Twin Trouble
My Precious Gift

Middlemarch Gathering
My Highland Mate
My Highland Fling

Middlemarch Capture
Snared by Saber
Favored by Felix
Lost with Leo
Spellbound with Sly
Journey with Joe
Star-Crossed with Scarlett